New York Times Bestselling Author
HELENA HUNTING

Randy Ballistic and Lily LeBlanc are head-over-heels, bed-breakingly, screaming orgasmically in love. But even they have their challenges, mostly outside of the bedroom.

With the off-season coming to a close and the boys gearing up for training camp, one more weekend of fun is the perfect way to welcome the new season.

The entire crew piles into vehicles and drives to Alex and Violet's Chicago cottage for a few days of relaxation—and hopefully a chance for Randy to shake the anxiety that's been plaguing him.

Accidental wardrobe malfunctions, typical Violet inspired overshares, and a whole lot of private time round out the perfect weekend getaway.

But the moment they return to the city all of Randy's angst resurfaces with the arrival of a surprise houseguest.

ACKNOWLEDGMENTS

Husband, you're my leading man. You make everything worth the effort.

Mom, Dad, Mel and Chris, your support means everything, so thank you for being so generous with it.

Deb, my sister wife in authoring; I love you a lot. We should be neighbors and not have to look at each other through a screen every day. We make crazy happen without even trying.

Kimberly, you know how much I love having you in my corner. Thank you for getting behind me and helping me through the fun stuff and the hard stuff.

My awesome team at RF and Bookcase—thank you for making wonderful things happen in other languages.

Nina; you will always wear the sparkle cape.

Jessica, there is no one quite like you. Honestly, I'm so lucky to have such a fabulous editor who makes me work harder and laugh my way through the crazy I sometimes throw at you.

Shannon, sweet lord this cover. Thank you for working your magic every time. You're such a rare talent.

Ellie and Franggy, this cover is beautiful because of you. Thank you so much.

Teeny, you're an awesome human. I love how beautiful you make the insides.

Erika, the broken ones are always the best.

Susi, muffin, man buns for the win.

Sarah—every author needs a right hand, one that isn't attached to their body but still manages to be just as important. That's you. Thank you for being so incredible. I could never keep track of my life the way you do.

Hustlers, you are incredibly amazing and wonderful and I love you. Thanks for the daily dose of beard to keep me breathing and inspired and thank you for always being there to celebrate the little things. Like Friday.

Beavers and Wood, I am so lucky to have all of you. Thank you for always keeping me entertained and feeling loved.

To my Backdoor Babes; Tara, Meghan, Deb and Katherine, every time we do something weird I think it's normal.

My Smut Saloon ladies; Melanie, Jessica and Geneva, there is nothing more exciting than remembering what we were supposed to do.

To my Pams, the Filets, my Nap girls; 101'ers, my Holiday's and Indies Tijan, Vi, Penelope, Susi, Deb, Erika, Katherine, Alice, Shalu, Amanda, Leisa, Kellie, Melissa, Sarah, Tracey, Teeny, you are fabulous in ways I can't explain. Thank you for being my friends, my colleagues, my supporters, my teachers, my cheerleaders and my soft places to land.

My WC crew; Angela, Jo, Gillian, Mandie, Peter, Jeremy, Cathy, John and Dave, thank you for celebrating this journey with me and for being my friends even though I don't get to see you every day anymore.

To all my author friends and colleagues; I'm so fortunate to have such an amazing support system in this crazy, awesome industry.

To all the amazing bloggers and readers out there who have supported me from the beginning of my angst, to the ridiculous of my humour; thank you for loving these stories, for giving them a voice, for sharing your thoughts and for being such amazing women. I'm honoured and humbled and constantly amazed by what a generous community you are.

To my Originals; my fandom friends who were with me back in the day when Wednesday postings were the way of things, thank you for giving me the gift of your feedback and your excitement. It's such an honour and a joy to know that you're still with me, on this road and that you're reason I took this journey in the first place.

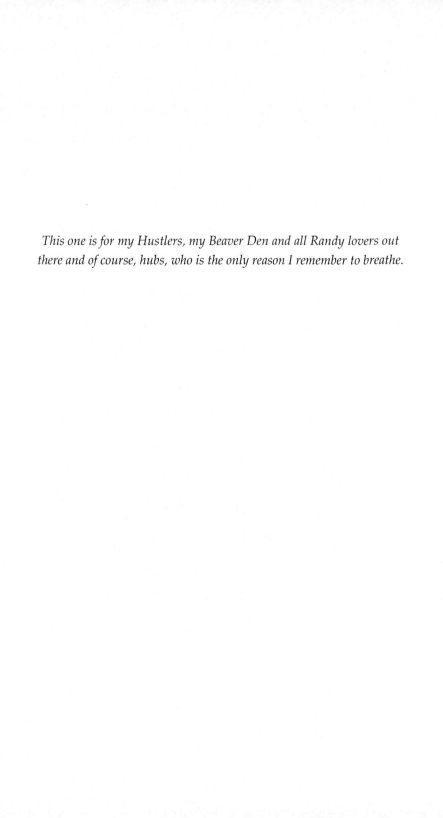

This one is for my Hustlers, my Beaver Den and all Randy lovers out there and of course, hubs, who is the only reason I remember to breathe.

THE SMELL OF ORGASMS

LILY

I prop my skate up on the bench to tighten the laces. After this session, my sexy, NHL-player boyfriend, Randy Ballistic, is picking me up for a weekend getaway with our friends. The cottage we're going to belongs to one of Randy's teammates, Alex Waters, who I've incidentally known my entire life since his younger sister, Sunny, is my best friend.

The off-season is about to come to an end, and training camp will start in less than two weeks. This last-hurrah weekend will be at Alex's Chicago cottage, not the Ontario cottage where Randy and I first met. As much as I'd love to revisit that location, any kind of weekend away with Randy and my friends is welcome, and this cottage is much closer.

With Sunny being pregnant, I'm sure things will be different

1

from the usual booze fest and overly late nights. Or maybe not—Alex's wife, Violet, and her friend Charlene Hoar are going to be there. Those two can drink like fish, and they like to stay up all hours of the night. I'm sure there will be dirty Scrabble games and shenanigans, both of which I'm looking forward to.

I'm not used to having this much down time. Prior to moving to Chicago, I'd always worked more than one job, so only having one means a lot more freedom to pursue hobbies. Not that I worry too much about being idle; Randy keeps me busy when I'm not teaching skating lessons. I don't have the opportunity to get bored—especially not since I moved in with him about four months ago and he enrolled me in beard riding classes.

I figured maybe once we were living together his insatiableness would wane, at least a little. It hasn't. While I've been teaching this morning, he's been texting me all the places he thinks we should have sex when we get to the cottage. Ironically, a bathroom hasn't even made the top five. The forest is a prime pick. He's mentioned playing hide and seek more than once, but the way he says it makes me think his version will be a lot different than the game I played with Sunny as a kid.

The door to the changing room squeaks as it opens. Someone needs to get out the WD-40 and deal with that. I'm around the corner, out of view, so I call out a hello to avoid scaring whoever it is. I get nothing back. A chill runs up my spine at the sound of distinctly non-feminine footfalls. Relief forces my heart back down from my throat when Randy peeks his head around the jamb.

"What're you doing in here?" I ask, double knotting my skate before lowering my foot to the rubber-padded floor.

He scans my outfit, and a devious grin pulls up the corner of his mouth. "Stopping in for a quick visit."

"In the women's staff locker room? What if someone else was in here with me?" It's a reasonable question. Occasionally I'm not the only instructor on the ice.

His eyes widen, and he checks over his shoulder. "Is there someone else here?"

"No. But there could've been."

"But you're telling me there isn't," he confirms.

I nod. "Still. What if you'd seen one of the other girls naked?"

He frowns and runs a hand over his beard, looking anxious. "I didn't think about that."

"Just imagine how embarrassed *I'd* be if someone else's boyfriend walked in while *I* was naked." Now I'm messing with him.

The furrow in his brow deepens, and his eyes go dark. If I didn't have a session in fifteen minutes, I'd be excited about that look, because it typically means very good things for the Vagina Emporium. Sadly, she's covered in multiple layers of fabric. And I'm hours away from any kind of relief for the ache that's flared low in my belly.

"Only I see you naked," Randy barks.

I snicker-snort. Sometimes Randy can be so very irrationally male.

He stalks forward to loom over me. "You think that's funny?"

"Someone else seeing me naked? No, I don't think that's funny at all. Your reaction to the unlikely possibility is, though. When we get to Alex's cottage, should we put you in a loincloth? We'll rename you a random sound, and you can club me over the head and drag me into the forest. We'll live in a cave, and you can battle bears to entertain me." I bite the inside of my cheek to hold in my laughter.

Randy cracks a sheepish grin. "That was pretty bad, wasn't it?"

"Uh, yeah."

He brushes a few strands of hair, imaginary or not, away from my cheek. "I'm a little greedy when it comes to you." He traces the edge of my jaw, the pad of his thumb sweeping my bottom lip.

"I'm aware."

3

Prior to me, Randy had seen lots of women naked. I thought I had a thick skin until I started dating him. As the girlfriend of an NHL player, I get personal messages from his former conquests about how they're a way better lay than I am, among other fun things. It was shocking at first, but at least I have friends who get what I'm going through.

I've had a total of five sexual partners, including Randy. I'm assuming Randy's had at least ten times that. Maybe it should bother me, but it doesn't. Now that we've decided to be together, he's never given me a reason to worry about him being unfaithful. His dad's history of cheating isn't one he wants to repeat.

"You still have a few minutes before you have to be on the ice, right?" he asks.

"I should get out there soon, but yeah."

Randy makes a noise but doesn't respond with words, which is sometimes his way. He's very much an action man. I knew he loved me a long time before he said the words out loud. All the little sacrifices, all the sweet things that come unprovoked are perfect examples of how he feels. And I feel the same way. But I don't think he's here to tell me he loves me. Not based on the gleam in his eye or the bulge making an appearance in his pants.

"What's up?" I pat the hard lump under the jeans. "Other than moody dick."

He covers my hand with his. "Wanna have a quickie?"

"I don't have enough minutes for that." I put my palm on his chest when he leans in. My resistance to Randy's advances is minimal, even with time constraints.

"I can be superfast. I bet you're halfway to coming already." A smirky grin tugs the side of his mouth. That smile used to infuriate me. Occasionally it still does.

Randy may be right; he has the incredible ability to get me off with very little physical contact. He's rather cocky about it. Being in a public locker room where someone could walk in any second should be a deterrent. But it really isn't—for either of us. Also, Randy takes much longer to come than I do. It's one of the positive side effects of the accident he had when he was a kid—the one that nearly robbed him of half of his amazing cock—and I have my doubts he'll be able to get off in under ten. His record is twelve minutes, and he was just crazy excited; it was the first time we went without a condom. Now he's gotten used to going in bare, so his longevity is astounding.

"There's no way you'll come before I have to get on the ice, and then we have to sit in a car with Sunny and Miller. You'll have to behave yourself for two hours with blue balls. How pleasant is that going to be for you?"

"I'm already gonna have blue balls, so it's not like it actually matters if I come. I can take care of myself after I take care of you."

I'm straddling the bench, so he plants a knee between my legs and leans forward. At the same time, he twines his fingers into the hair at the nape of my neck, angling my head back as if he's planning to kiss me.

"You can't wait until we get to the cottage to get me off?" It's taking a superhuman amount of self-restraint not to shift against his strategically placed knee.

"I can, but I don't *want* to." He drops his head so his mouth is close to mine. "Come on, luscious. You send me all these pictures of you in your skating gear; now you're gonna deny me what you've been enticing me with for the past four hours?"

He smells fantastic, like the cologne I bought him for Valentine's Day. "You asked for those pictures."

"I know. Now I want to thank you for them by making you come."

"How are you planning to make me come?" It's a challenge to remember why this isn't a great idea with him looking so good and talking about giving me orgasms.

"How 'bout with my fingers?"

"I'm fully dressed."

"Like that's ever stopped me before."

He has a point. He can make me come just by rubbing up on me. Our chemistry is ridiculous.

I finally give in when he kisses me. I should feel bad that I'm about to receive an orgasm at work, in the changing room, but Randy's good at persuasion, and providing pleasure, so it's hard to feel anything other than excitement.

He brings his knee forward, and I start grinding on him right away.

I can hear his smile. "That's it; take what you want, baby."

I nip at his lip, aware he's playing with me. I'll get him back later. He slips his tongue in my mouth and starts a slow, stroking rhythm that in no way matches the slightly desperate way I'm grinding against his knee. Randy has that effect. He knows it, and he likes to use it to his advantage.

His hand stays where it is, cradling my head as we kiss. I keep rolling my hips, wishing he was hitting my special spot with a more precise body part, such as the fingers he talked about. I reach between us and palm him—he's extra hard—through his pants. Now I wish actual sex was an option not impeded by the barrier of clothing, which I'm beginning to think is part of his master plan.

Randy enjoys getting me all amped up and then leaving me hanging—well, not totally. I always get to come, but he won't, and I don't like the inequity in that. I'm already close though, so I'll make it work until we have the opportunity to do this naked. With more privacy. Just as the tingles begin to spread, Randy backs off. I groan and grab for his belt buckle, but he breaks the kiss and puts one wide palm on the center of my chest, urging me to lie back on the bench.

"What're you doing? I was almost there." I'm snappy. It makes him smile.

"I said I was gonna use my fingers." He pushes them under the elastic of my leotard and skims the hot, damp skin between my legs, still barred by a pair of tights and panties. The palm on my chest moves lower, his fingertips gliding over my left breast and down my stomach. When he reaches the leg hole, he slips that hand under as well.

Finding the waistband of my tights, he yanks them roughly over my hips, pulling them down until they reach the crotch of my skating outfit. Then he goes back for my panties and does the same.

"Do you have any idea how often I think about fucking you like this?"

Randy has a thing for my skating outfits, as evidenced by our current situation. We've had sex while I'm wearing one of my competition leotards—the kind with all the sequins and decorative crap. There weren't any panties or tights to get in the way, though. It was just a matter of moving the crotch to the side and getting in there. That sex was insane.

"I assume it's a daily thing," I say snarkily.

"You assume correctly." He shifts the material so he can access my Vagina Emporium. Threads strain and snap.

"Careful." I don't want my outfit totally stretched out in the name of an orgasm.

"I'll buy you a new one when I wreck this."

I note there's no *if*. "I don't have a spare here."

Randy is either too focused on getting his fingers where he wants them, or he's ignoring me. I assume it's a combination of the two. He caresses my clit with the back of his fingers as he tries to make room for his hand. I gasp and bite my lip to stifle my moan. The walls in here are cinderblock and great for acoustics, not so great for covert orgasms.

He fumbles around in his back pocket, producing his phone.

I prop myself up on an elbow. "Seriously? You need to do that right now?"

"You actually need to ask that question? This is like…" A few facial tics follow, and he opens and closes his mouth before the words finally come. "If they actually made figure-skating porn, I'd have a real problem."

"I think you already have a real problem."

7

Randy disregards my sassitude and hits the record button. "This woman right here is my number-one fantasy, and she's all mine." He maneuvers his hand in the limited space between my panties and tights, which are cutting into my thighs, they're stretched so tight.

"But only for the next ten minutes," I add.

He pushes two fingers inside and offers a low "fuck, yeah."

I bow up off the bench; the loud tearing sound should concern me, but he does the finger curl. Then he drops his head and suctions himself to my clit. This is fairly atypical behavior for Randy. Usually he's a tongue-only kind of tease with the eating out, so he must be going for maximum effect. I honestly try not to come right away, but he has all the control over my body, so I freefall into orgasm heaven. I bang my head on the bench and bring my hand to my mouth, biting the side of it to muffle my moans.

Randy doesn't stop sucking even after I've come. Instead he keeps going, aware he'll be able to make me come a second time with minimal effort. Usually he gives me a short reprieve, though, allowing me to come down from the high before he sets me off again. Not so this time.

Tears pool and run down my temples at the pleasure-pain. My entire body jerks and trembles as orgasm number two bitch-slaps me. When my motor function returns, I shove my fingers in his hair and yank, disconnecting his mouth from my oversensitive clit.

He makes this low sound, kind of a growl, like he's pissed that I've stopped him.

"Jesus, Randy, what's gotten into you?" A full-body tremor—like a legitimate aftershock—makes me lose my grip on his hair.

His expression softens and then becomes panicked. "Lily? Shit."

The fullness of his fingers inside me disappears. My muscles contract around nothing and an odd, soft sob gets caught in my throat. He reaches out as if to caress my cheek, but realizes my

8

orgasm is still all over his fingers, so he wipes his hand on his shirt. At least it's white.

He leans over me, sweeping shaky fingers across my temple. His eyes are wide, his thick swallow audible. "Did I hurt you? Are you okay? I didn't mean to get carried away. I just wanted to make you feel good."

I still his hands. "You didn't hurt me."

"But you're crying. I made you cry. That's not supposed to happen."

"You wouldn't let me stop coming. It was intense." I motion to my face. "These aren't pain tears, they're overwhelmed-by-sensation tears."

"Oh." His relief leaves him on an exhale. "I didn't know that was a thing. So you're telling me you can come so hard you cry?"

I'm actually surprised this has never happened to him before. His orgasm missions, along with his former reputation with the bunnies, are legendary.

There's something going on with Randy. He's been extra needy lately. Only once this week have we not had sex multiple times a day. Maybe he's stocking up in preparation for being on the road again once the new season starts. I'm not complaining; I just think there's more to it than him being horny. The alarm on my phone goes off. It's my final warning.

"Oh, God. I need to fix myself and get out there!"

"Told you I could get you off before you went on the ice." The smug tone is there, but he's missing the usual smirky smirk.

My legs are wobbly as I stand and adjust my panties, then my stretched-out tights. The waistband on both are shot. They'll have to go in the garbage after this. Also, a huge snag runs from waist to thigh on my right leg. I don't have an extra pair of tights with me, so I'll have to deal. The crotch of my leotard is loose now, too, which definitely isn't optimal—especially since I'm about to teach pairs. I haven't done pairs in years, so I'm relearning a bit as I'm teaching.

Tonight I have a one-on-one session with Finlay to work on some of the lifts. Last session his partner, Giselle, twisted her ankle, so she's taking some time to recover. I didn't want Finlay to miss this session, though.

I look up at Randy and gesture to my outfit. "Thanks a lot; this whole thing is ruined now."

"I'll take you to get new ones."

"Hell of a lot of good that's going to do me now."

"I'm sorry." He jams his hands in his pockets and rocks back on his heels. "I got excited thinking about the cottage and spending time with you without work getting in the way."

I don't want him to feel bad for making me feel good. I share his enthusiasm, even if his timing could be better. I put a hand on his chest and give him a quick kiss. "I know. Me too. I gotta go, though."

I close my locker and head for the ice on unsteady legs in a skating outfit that fit a lot better less than ten minutes ago. I catch a glimpse of myself in the mirror before I push through the doors to the rink. My hair is all messed up in the back, so I quickly finger-comb it. My tights are sliding down because the waistband is so loose. My cheeks are flushed, my lips swollen, my eyes bright. I can smell Randy's cologne all over me, and I'm pretty sure I also smell like an orgasm, but that could all be in my head.

There's nothing I can do about it now. I'm annoyed that I look like such an unprofessional mess, but hopefully Finlay is too focused on learning the routine to notice.

He's already out there when I hit the ice. Finlay turned nineteen recently and has been skating competitively since he was a child. He's an incredible skater, but I know he's worried about the lifts and the jumps. Since I know this routine, my boss called in a favor and asked if I would be willing to coach him and his partner. They've already made state, and now they're looking at nationals. Those two are magic together when they're on. It's an honor and a big deal to be asked to do this. Summer hours mean I have the time, so I couldn't say no.

Finlay looks antsy. He's been great, if not a little unsure of himself, the two times I've worked with him and Giselle so far. I've heard he can be a bit of a perfectionist, and hard on himself and his partner in terms of expectations. I'm hoping this session will help keep things smooth and easy between them. He's feeling some guilt over Giselle's minor injury, even though it wasn't his fault.

He glances at the clock. I'm two minutes late. "I thought maybe I got the time wrong."

"Sorry. One of my laces broke; I had to relace with a spare." The lie comes smoothly.

He looks down at my skates, eyes moving over my outfit. My freaking tights are already falling down. Randy's going to hear it from me later.

I clap my hands together. "I guess we should warm up."

"I was a little early. I've already warmed up."

"I meant together. I've been on the ice all day, so I'm about as warmed up as I'm going to get, but I'm happy to do a few laps to get us in the groove."

"Oh, right. Yeah, of course." He bobble nods. "That sounds like a good idea."

I skate a tight circle around him and then speed off down the ice, adjusting my damn tights. At least the little skirt covers some of the issue. I'm kind of nervous about this session. It's one thing to teach other people how to skate together; it's totally different when I'm the one involved in the togetherness. Pairs requires a lot of trust and communication. It's been a long time since I've had to skate with another person. And now, on top of dealing with the newness of this situation, my attention is divided because my tights keep sliding down, and all I can think about is how that happened. Goddamn Randy and his magic tongue and fingers.

Still, all I have to do is invest an hour, and then I'm free for the weekend.

After a few laps around the rink, the guy in the sound booth cues the music, and we start the routine. Finlay has the first part down, but whenever he has to make physical contact, he gets all twitchy and unsure of himself, especially when there's a lift.

"Are you okay today?" I ask when he fumbles me for the third time.

"Uh, yeah, just…there's a guy in the stands, and he's been watching us for, like, ten minutes. He looks really familiar."

I look around the arena and spot Randy sitting in the stands.

Randy rarely stays to watch me, and I have a feeling it's no coincidence he's decided to stick around while I'm teaching Finlay. His neediness this week, his sneaking into the locker room, the "impromptu" orgasms he couldn't wait to give me, my smelling like I've doused myself in his cologne—all this leads me to believe his behavior is orchestrated and intentional. And I don't know quite what to make of that.

When the song ends, I suggest we take a short break and grab some water.

Finlay looks to where my problematic boyfriend is sitting. "That guy totally looks like Randy Ballistic."

I roll my eyes. "That's because he is."

His eyes go wide. "Holy shit. What's he doing here?"

"Being a pain in my ass."

"Huh?"

"He's my boyfriend."

I almost enjoy his shock. "Wow. I wasn't sure if that was a rumor or not." He gestures between us, looking understandably nervous. "So is this a problem?"

"No. He's waiting because he doesn't have anything better to do. I'll be right back."

I skate over to Randy, because I'm not exactly sure it isn't a problem, based on what happened in the changing room. He's reclining in a chair one row back from the boards with his arm slung casually across the seat next to him. He flashes me a smile that's anything but easy.

I point a finger at him as soon as I'm close enough. "I'm on to you."

His eyes flare slightly before he cocks his head to the side, giving me his signature grin. "On to me? It's not like I was hiding out. I'm just watch—"

I cut him off. "Don't even think about lying."

He opens his mouth and then closes it. Speechless Randy is new. He has a quick retort for just about everything.

I take advantage of his silence. "Yes or no, you ambushed me in the locker room so I'd smell like you and orgasms when I came out here to practice with Finlay."

"What kind of name is Finlay, anyway?"

"That's not a yes or a no."

He runs a hand over his beard and mumbles something.

I crook a finger. "C'mere."

He regards me with something like chagrin before he unfurls from his seated position. Randy's a big man. He's well over six feet tall, broad and weighing in at more than two hundred pounds during the off-season. He has to work hard to keep that weight on during game season because he burns calories faster than he can consume them. He may look intimidating to some, but he's not to me.

He jumps the seats to stand in the first row. Only the boards separate us. His tongue peeks out to wet his bottom lip as he looks me over. I have to adjust my tights for the eleven-millionth time. If I had to guess, I'd say he's hard. He likes me feisty.

"I didn't quite catch that," I say softly.

Randy grips the boards, his fingertips going white as his gaze lifts over my head, likely to my skating partner, before it settles on me again. "Can you blame me?"

"Blame you for what exactly?"

"Wanting you to smell like me."

I totally called it. "So you're aiming for twenty-first-century

13

caveman, now? Is this your version of peeing on a tree to mark your territory?"

He frowns. "Dogs do that, not cavemen. Or evolved cavemen, like me, apparently."

I prop a fist on my hip. "You know what I mean. It's the same thing."

"It's not even remotely the same."

He's being antagonistic on purpose. He knows it gets me hot. Right now I'm legitimately irritated, though. And I'm offended that it seems a lot like he doesn't trust me. Although, now isn't really the time to have it out about trust issues. "We're not arguing about this now."

"I didn't realize it was an argument at all. That guy has his hands all over you. We have sex to this song all the damn time. I think it's reasonable for me to want him to know you're not available."

I didn't even consider how often we get it on to the song. "And you thought the best way to accomplish that was by eating me out in the locker room ten minutes before I had to be on the ice with him?"

"You seemed to enjoy yourself."

My magic marble agrees. "That's beside the point. We'll be talking about this later."

"That sounds like a good idea. You can tell me exactly what you liked best about my eating your pussy in the changing room and if there's anything you'd want me to do differently next time."

"I'm not kidding."

"Neither am I. I take eating your pussy very seriously." Randy manages not to crack a smile. "Wanna introduce me to *Finlay*?"

"So he can run when he sees you coming for him?"

"Pretty much."

GET OFF
MY GIRL

RANDY

S o maybe I'm being somewhat unreasonable, but I'm also still new at the girlfriend thing. And this guy seems like a dick. Or maybe that's me being overprotective of what's mine. Not that Lily is a possession, but she's my girlfriend, and I don't want anyone putting the moves on her. Especially not this guy. I did some research before I decided I should stay and watch Lily skate. Apparently Finlay has had a relationship with his last two skating partners. I get that Lily is his instructor, not his partner, but today is a one-on-one session. I want to make sure he's aware that she's not a viable dating option.

It's not that I don't trust Lily. I do. She's more than capable of taking care of herself, but I don't ever want her to be in a position where that's a problem. She's gorgeous, and talented. I get a little nervous. I'm also a whole lot stressed about the beginning of the season and being away from her for extended periods of time. I've gotten used to being home with her, seeing her every day. The upcoming season is going to be an adjustment.

Lily motions for the guy to come over so she can do the introduction thing. He's shorter than me by a good four inches, and I definitely outweigh him by at least forty pounds. Based on what his spandex business doesn't hide, I'm also way more equipped to take care of Lily's needs in the bedroom.

"Be nice," Lily hisses.

I extend a hand and smile instead of punching him in the face. I need to get a handle on this jealousy. "Hey, I'm Randy."

"Hey, hi. Finlay." He takes my offered palm.

"I'm Lily's boyfriend. She lives with me. In my house."

Lily makes a sound like she's choking, or coughing, or both. I glance at her. I don't think that was the right thing to say.

"Right. Okay." Finlay blinks and swallows. "I, uh, I read that somewhere—"

Lily slaps a palm on the boards. "We should probably get back to it." She gives me an overly sweet, somewhat annoyed smile. "You know what I'd love?"

Judging from her tone, I don't think it's another changing-room orgasm. "What's that, luscious?"

"A tea."

"You want me to get you one from the concession stand?"

She makes a face. "The tea here sucks. Oh! I'd like a chai latte. There's a Starbucks down the street. It's, like, a ten-minute walk. You don't mind, do you? Finlay, do you want anything?"

Finlay looks uncomfortable. "Uh, no. I'm good. Thanks."

Clearly Lily's trying to get rid of me, which means I've definitely said the wrong thing. I tried to be nice. Okay, maybe I didn't try that hard, but I can make up for it with food. "You want anything besides a chai latte? I can get you one of those oat bar things you like."

"That'd be great." This time her smile holds less tension.

I lean in to kiss her, but she gives me her cheek. I back off, and when she turns her head, I manage to connect her mouth with mine. The PDA must be too much for Finlay because he says something about it being nice to meet me and skates away.

"Did you even wash your face?" she whispers when he's out of hearing range.

This time I don't bother to hold back my grin. "Why? Can you smell yourself on me?"

"You're unbelievable. What about your hands? Please tell me you washed those."

I hold a finger up under my nose and then offer it to her. "Wanna check?"

"Oh my God. No." She bats it away.

"Smells like luscious lilies."

"You have a problem."

"What can I say? I'm an addict."

"You're insane is what you are. Go get me a latte. You're making Finlay nervous."

"Good. That's exactly what I want him to be." I consider how my presence might affect Lily in this situation. "Am I making you nervous?"

"No. Just harder to do my job."

"Horny?"

"No."

"You sure?"

She pushes on my chest. "Can you go? You're such a distraction."

I take her hand and kiss her fingers. "Are you mad at me?"

"The jury's still out on that. Now go, and don't rush back." She pulls her hand from my grip and skates off, flipping me the bird behind her back. She also has to adjust her tights, which means she draws attention to her ass. That would be fine if it was just me checking it out, but I'm about to leave, which means Finlay will have plenty of opportunity to stare at it while I'm gone. Damn it.

I want to be back to the rink as fast as possible, even though Lily doesn't seem to want me there, so I take my truck instead of walking. It only takes two minutes to drive to Starbucks. But it's the kind with no drive thru, so I end up having to circle the block and find a spot down the street.

There must be some kind of event going on nearby, or a fucking field trip, because the place is packed with people—and not just with the usual laptop-toters. There's a huge line waiting to order and a sizable group congregated at the counter, still waiting for their drinks. I get asked for an autograph three times, and of course there are subsequent selfies to be had.

By the time I get back in my truck, Lily's session with that Finlay fucker is already over. Fucking tourists and their frappe-lappa-what-the-fuck-evers and their ridiculous indecision. When I'm back at the arena I check the rink anyway, in case they're still there, but it's now filled with little kids bumbling around. I head for the changing room to find the door locked.

Shit.

I really hope she isn't super pissed at me. That would not be a good way to start our weekend. Particularly since I'm hoping it will contain a high amount of nudity and sex.

I stand in the hall, holding her latte and an oat bar—plus a muffin because Lily is always hungry—and wait. And wait some more. My phone buzzes, so I check to see if she's messaging. It's Miller, wondering when we're going to be there. I send him a voice memo saying we'll be on our way soon.

Then I text Lily to let her know I'm waiting on the other side of the locked door.

As soon as it opens, I step forward and force her back in. "Are we alone in here?"

"Yes, but you're not pulling that stunt on me again."

I close the door and lock it, which makes it look like I'm trying to do exactly that. I'm not.

"I'm sorry." I set the latte down and take her face in my hands.

Then I kiss her. I don't attempt tongue. She might bite me. Instead I wrap my arms around her and hug the shit out of her. She wriggles at first, but then she just stands there. After another minute she gives in and hugs me back. I turn my face into her neck and drop a kiss there, then another on her jaw, and one on her cheek. She lets me get as far as her lips, but when I add a little tongue, she puts a hand on either side of my face and disengages our mouths.

She purses her plush lips until they're a straight line. "I thought you said you were okay with me teaching pairs."

"I am okay with you teaching pairs."

"Really? Because the locker room pussy diving and flag pole territory-claiming indicate you're not."

"I wanted to meet him."

She gives me a look.

"Do you know the history on this guy? He's had relationships with his last two partners." Honestly, when she said she was teaching pairs, I didn't stop to think that part of it would be demonstrating moves with the fucking dude before he tried them on the other chick.

"But I'm not his partner. And I'm with you, so that's not relevant anyway. How do you even know that about him?"

"I read it somewhere. And you're his instructor, which makes you, like, his number-one wet dream. I bet he wants to bone you more than he does his partner."

"Did you internet stalk him?" she asks, sounding incredulous.

"No. I read a couple of articles because I was curious, and I wanted to see what he looked like—I mean, who you were working with." I'm digging myself a deeper hole with all this honesty crap.

"First of all, he's my student."

"Yeah, but he's nineteen."

"He still has acne, and he probably only has to shave once a week. Secondly, I already have a seriously hot boyfriend.

Thirdly, he's not even remotely as attractive as you are. On a scale of one to ten, you're a twelve, and he's maybe a—"

"Two?" I offer.

"I was going to be nice and say six."

I can tell she's trying to appease me even though she's still kind of mad.

"So that's what this whole set-up was about today? Me teaching pairs and you needing to make sure my student knows you're my boyfriend? And that I live with you, in your house?"

"I figured that was pushing the line. I'm sorry."

"I don't want you to be sorry. I want you to trust me."

"I do trust you. It's the nineteen-year-old bag of hormones I don't trust." I take a deep breath and decide to come clean. "My sister called this morning. I think she's, like, homesick but doesn't want to come out and say it. I'm kinda worried about her. The season's starting soon, and my dad called last week for the first time in months. Those conversations are always uplifting, and he called again today saying he might be in the area. I don't feel like dealing with him, and then there's this pairs thing. It's great, and I totally support this because you're amazing on the ice, but I didn't realize this guy was gonna get to put his hands on you for, like, an extended period of time and, like, touch you and shit, and that fucking song is *our* song, and I don't want him to touch you." Jesus. I sound like a controlling dick. Maybe I am. I really fucking hope not.

"Oh, baby." Lily strokes my beard, and her fingertips brush over my lips.

It's not the reaction I expected.

"Is Brynne okay? It can't be easy with her so far away."

"I don't know. There's gotta be more going on than she's telling me. I hate that she's all the way in Australia; I can't do anything. I'm not awesome with the talking, as you know."

"You're better than you think."

"I don't know about that. Fuck. I'm sorry I was a dick."

"You weren't a dick…maybe a little possessive and ridiculous." She stresses the *dick* in ridiculous and gets a smile out of me.

Lily pushes up on her toes and runs her hands through my hair. Her touch is gentle, soothing. It's what I need. She's what I need. Sometimes it makes me nervous how much. Like now. And earlier when she was skating with that guy to our song.

"Why didn't you tell me your dad called?"

"It puts me in a bad mood. I figured it wasn't worth mentioning."

Lily sighs. "You can tell me these things, Randy. You don't have to keep this stuff to yourself."

"I know. I just… I get worried."

"Worried about what?"

"He was talking about coming to Chicago this weekend."

"Did you tell him we were going to be away?"

"I mentioned I wouldn't be in town." But that doesn't stop him from wanting a place to crash. I could manage that before, but not with Lily living with me. He's grown progressively worse over the past couple of years—making a mess, being a big dick.

Sometimes it's hard to be honest. I'm not accustomed to having these truthful conversations about feelings. I haven't really expressed how much it worries me that I'm going to be on the road. And my dad's recent phone calls haven't helped. He's also mentioned the girlfriend rumors, and I haven't told him about Lily. But then if he bothered to check the media, he'd know anyway.

When I talked to him last week, he was full of his usual little digs about my playing, about how I handle myself off the ice, about my mom—just everything. And he gets to me; he gets in my head and makes me question what I can and can't handle. I hate it.

Squeezing my eyes shut, I shove down the negative thoughts. I just want this weekend with my girlfriend without any issues.

I take in Lily's outfit. She's wearing a sundress. She's definitely braless; I know because the dress is strapless, and she doesn't bother with bras unless they're absolutely necessary. The top of the dress is all gathered and elastic-y. I could pull it right down, and she'd be in her panties in a second.

I run a finger from one collarbone to the other. "Lily." Her name comes out all gravelly and low. I'm sure my expression tells her more than words will.

"What can I do to make this easier for you?"

I shrug and ease my finger under the elastic. This time I skim the swell of her breast. I'm pretty close to a nipple.

"You want a distraction from what's going on in your head?" she asks.

This is one of the reasons I love her. She calls me out on my bullshit, and then makes it better.

"It might help."

She drops her bag on the floor and pulls my mouth to hers. She fumbles with my belt one-handed while I tug her dress down. Once it reaches her thighs, it drops to the floor and pools at her feet.

I grab her hips, searching for panties to remove. "Where's your underwear?"

"In my bag. I wanted to be prepared. I had a feeling something was going on." Her hand goes down the front of my boxers. I'm wearing my favorite pair; the ones she defaced almost a year ago when we first met at Waters' Ontario cottage. They say *Tiny Dick Inside*. That's a lie. There's nothing tiny about me.

"I love how good you are to me." I groan when she wraps her fingers around my cock. Turning, I lift her by the waist. Lily wraps her legs around me, and I pin her to the wall with my body. We're all lined up and ready for fucking.

"You need a primer, or are you good to go?" I ask.

"I've been primed for the past hour."

I take her mouth again and ease inside her. Her eyes roll up and she hums, like my being in her is a relief we both need. She's hot and tight and naked, and I'm still fully dressed, but that doesn't matter. Later, when we get to Waters' cottage, we can both be naked, and I'll take more time with her, show her how much I appreciate what she's giving me right now.

"All the doors are locked?"

"Yup."

"So you pretty much called it that I'd come back looking for more of you?"

"You're always looking for more of me."

She's not being cocky. It's true.

She clasps her hands behind my neck. "It's your turn to take what you need, baby."

So I do. Because she lets me. Because I love her. Because she loves me back.

BY THE TIME I'm done with the taking, and the giving, we both have messages. Lily's are from Sunny, and mine are from Miller. We both message back to let them know we're on our way—for real this time.

Alex and another of my teammates, Darren Westinghouse, are already at Sunny and Miller's place with Violet and Charlene by the time we get there.

"Neither one of you is allowed to use the bathroom before we leave," Violet says by way of greeting.

"I've already taken care of Randy; he should be good until we get to the cottage," Lily replies with a sweet smile.

I chuckle and kiss the top of her hair.

"Road head?" Violet asks.

"Nope." Lily's smile widens until she hides it behind her latte cup. It's probably cold by now, but she doesn't seem to care.

Sunny wrinkles her nose. "Please tell me you did not have sex in a Starbuck's bathroom."

"God, no. Those are gross. We had locker room wall sex," Lily says.

Violet's eyes light up. "Oooh! High five. The locker rooms in the arenas are so clean. I remember when Alex got kicked out of that game and I went to find him. That was some seriously hot sex." She turns to Waters. "We should do that again. Except let's not get caught this time."

"Uh, yeah, I don't think we're gonna do that again, and if this is the kind of conversation you plan on having, I vote you girls drive together," he says.

"What he said." Westinghouse points at Waters.

"Sunny's not going with the girls if Violet's driving." Miller gives her belly a protective pat.

Violet puts her hands on her hips and pushes her chest out. She's wearing a tank top that says AWESOME across her boobs. They really don't need the extra attention. "I'm not that bad of a driver."

That gets a round of throat clearing.

She looks around at the group. "Oh, come on, I've only had two little fender benders."

"This year," Miller says.

"You backed your car into an eight-foot fence last week," Charlene points out.

"I didn't see it!"

"Because you weren't paying attention," Sunny says.

"Because there was a spider on my windshield!" Violet protests.

"Lily can drive my truck, and we'll take the SUV." If we hadn't just had sex in the changing room, I wouldn't be so open to this arrangement, but maybe a couple hours of girl-bonding time will minimize the number of really fucking weird conversations they need to have after we're all together.

"See?" Violet turns to Alex and gestures between me and Lily. "Balls lets Lily drive his truck, and I bet she doesn't even have to bribe him with blow jobs."

Miller holds up his hand. "Save the BJ convos for the car ride. And Randy lets Lily drive his truck because she doesn't run into stationary objects. Can we get a move on? I wanna be on the road before rush hour hits." He turns to Sunny and rubs her rounded stomach. "Sunny Sunshine, you need to hit the bathroom before we roll out?"

"It's probably a good idea."

The rest of us pile into the vehicles while Sunny makes one last bathroom trip. Apparently being eight months pregnant means you have to pee a lot more often. I've been warned that we may need to stop on the way. In addition to the people, we have Titan and Andy, Sunny's dogs, along for the ride, plus an extra they're fostering because Sunny had a weak moment. They're calling him Wiener because he's a wiener dog. Titan is a tiny little Papillon, and he's riding with the girls, along with the wiener, but Andy is a huge Dane, so he's riding in the SUV with us.

Miller makes Sunny sit in the backseat because he thinks it's safer. Then he settles into the SUV and proceeds to text her every five minutes for the first half hour of the trip to make sure she's okay. We can see the truck right next to us on the highway.

"Dude, Lily's an excellent driver, Sunny'll be fine," I reassure him.

"I know." He pockets his phone and taps on the armrest.

Sunny getting pregnant wasn't planned, but Miller seems to be dealing with it pretty well. It's weird to think about him becoming a dad when a little more than a year ago he was notorious with the bunnies. He's a little overprotective, but I guess that makes sense. Lily and I were the first ones to find out about it. It was a huge shock, and there was some family drama— Waters wasn't all that excited at first—but things are good now. For a couple of weeks after Sunny got knocked up, Lily and I went back to using condoms out of sheer paranoia.

It lasted two boxes, and then we were back to bag-free sex— because we ran out in the middle of the night and neither of us was willing to settle for oral. Lily's been on the pill for a long time, and she's really good about taking them at the same time every day, so we've relaxed about the whole thing. I still have no desire to get her pregnant—her mother might actually kill me if that happened. Right now Lily's mom likes me, and I want to keep it that way.

An hour into the drive, we stop so Sunny can pee again. We all get out to stretch our legs while Waters gasses up the SUV. Miller heads directly for the washroom, presumably to check on Sunny. The amount he worries about her makes me question the whole parenting thing, possibly at any point.

Lily and I have been dating for less than a year. I'm good with the living-together deal, and she seems to be too. We're both young, and we come from broken families. Statistically that doesn't put us in the best position. But I try not to dwell on that too much, because it's a shitty way to think.

I find Lily at the checkout of the convenience store with an armload of snacks. She deposits them on the counter as I pull out my phone to snap a couple of pics of her. I lean down and press a kiss to her shoulder, then run my nose up the side of her neck, snapping photo after photo the entire time. If I printed them out, it'd be like a flip book. The teenage boy behind the cash register looks away.

"You fueling up so you're ready for me later?" I whisper in her ear.

Lily giggles. "Sunny's hungry, and she can't decide what she wants, so I stocked up on some of everything."

I point to the bag of Doritos. "I'd appreciate it if you didn't eat any of those, unless your plan is to make your breath so bad I don't want to kiss you for the rest of the weekend."

"Those are for Charlene."

"She mad at Darren or something?"

"Doesn't seem like it, but you never know what's up with those two."

"Mmm." I don't really get that relationship. They've been

together almost as long as Waters and Violet, but it still seems pretty casual. Westinghouse is hard to get a read on. He's a quiet guy, and private. He and Waters are tight, which is why we hang out, but I still don't know all that much about him.

I pull my wallet from my back pocket, find my credit card, and toss it on the counter.

Lily snatches it up before the cashier does. "I can get this."

"I know you can, but I'm gonna steal that bag of gummy bears and the Twizzlers too, so I'd feel bad about you paying for those. Just let me get it, luscious, please."

Lily gives me a look, but she passes back the card, and I hand it to the kid. Sometimes it's hard for her to deal with me paying for things all the time. But I have the money, and while her job pays well, relatively speaking, it's got nothing on my salary. I try not to make it a thing, but she's got pride, and she doesn't want a free ride. I understand that and appreciate it. It doesn't mean I don't want to spoil the fuck out of her anyway. I just find more subversive ways to do it.

"Thank you," she says softly.

"You don't need to thank me for stealing your candy." I nibble on her shoulder.

The chime of the door opening reminds me we're not alone.

"For the love of PDA, give this poor kid a break." Violet gestures to the cashier, who has turned a bright shade of red. "Do you two need ten minutes in the forest before we hit the road, or do you think you can make it another hour?"

I back up off Lily. "We'll manage."

"Just making sure. Oh! You got me Swedish Fish! I love you, Lily Pad!" Violet pushes her way between us and drapes an arm over Lily's shoulder.

"Call me that again and I'll eat the entire bag in front of you, and I won't share," Lily snaps.

Violet raises her hands. "Sorry. I thought it was cute. Maybe not?"

Based on Lily's comment, I'm going with *not*, which means

I'm going to call her that later tonight in bed, just to get her all fired up.

The kid behind the counter packs the snacks into a bag.

Violet nabs the chips. "Who asked for these?"

"Charlene."

She frowns and looks over her shoulder to the parking lot. Charlene is sitting sideways in the truck, and Darren's standing between her legs. They appear to be having a conversation.

"I guess it's her prerogative if she only wants it doggy-style this weekend."

The kid behind the counter coughs.

I finish paying for the goods, and we all head back out to the vehicles. Violet tosses the bag of Doritos to Charlene, whose eyes widen as Darren's expression darkens. He says one last thing to her and steps back. Shifting her legs so they're back in the truck, he closes the door. The window's open, so she grabs his sleeve before he can walk away. He doesn't look particularly amused as he turns back to her, but he sticks his head in the window.

"I seriously wonder what the deal is there," I say.

Lily threads her fingers through mine. "Yeah. Me, too."

"I hope they're not gonna fight all weekend."

"I don't know that they fight." She kisses my bicep.

"What do you call that?" I incline my head in their direction.

"I think it's a game, like cat and mouse. I just can't figure out who's the cat and who's the mouse."

It's an interesting observation. But I still hope it's not a sign of what the rest of the weekend is going to be like. I don't need their weird drama affecting my good time.

HOW TO REVIVE
A BOYFRIEND

LILY

As I approach, Darren walks away from the truck holding the bag of Doritos. He's smirking, which is uncommon for him. I glance at Charlene to find she's wearing a similar look. I don't ask, because I'm not sure I want to know what the fascination is with Doritos. To my knowledge, all they do is make your breath horrible.

Back on the road, Violet sits beside me, fiddling with the music while Sunny rifles through the snacks and tries one of everything—apart from the beef jerky, which is mine. She's kind enough to open the bag for me, though. That's new. In addition to not touching or eating meat, Sunny usually opens a window when meat products are nearby, as if the molecules will somehow infiltrate her body through smell.

29

Violet gives up on finding a clear station and chooses a playlist on her phone. It's The Tragically Hip, my favorite Canadian band—perfect cottage music.

She turns to Charlene. "So what's the deal with the Doritos?"

"Huh?" Charlene stops fingering her necklace and looks up from her phone.

"Why would you want to ruin your weekend by eating Doritos? Or is Darren a bad kisser and that's your way of making sure you don't have to make out with him?"

"Darren's an excellent kisser."

"Uh-huh. Sure. So why the stinky-breath chips?" Violet asks.

"They aren't in the truck, are they?" Sunny looks concerned.

"Darren took them," I say.

"Oh. That's good. Otherwise I'd want to eat them, and then I wouldn't be able to make out with Miller later, and that would be sad." Sunny blinks a few times, like she's fighting tears.

Pregnancy has made her extra emotional. Lately she's been crying at bathroom tissue commercials. And her volunteer position at the SPCA has resulted in the foster wiener dog snuggled up beside me. He's so freaking cute, but they already have two dogs, and a baby on the way. I don't know that they need more things to take care of.

"I guess you're not getting your freak on all that often anymore, what with the volleyball you're packing," Violet muses.

"We only have sex five or six times a week now," Sunny says wistfully.

"Only?" Charlene seems shocked.

"Miller likes morning sex, and I like night sex, so we switch back and forth. Except we take a day off a week. That's Miller's cookie-eating day."

Violet opens her mouth and then shuts it. Her cheeks puff out. She gestures to Sunny's tummy. "I just—isn't it uncomfortable?"

Sunny pats her stomach. "Well, we can't really do missionary anymore, but Miller knows how to make me feel good."

"Amen to that, sister!" Charlene gives her a high five.

"Says the woman who was planning to eat a bag of Doritos," Violet points out.

"I was never going to eat them. I wanted Darren to think I was. Sex tonight is going to be amazing." Charlene has a wicked gleam in her eye.

Violet shakes her head. "And you think I'm weird."

"You dress up Alex's dick like a superhero; you are weird," Charlene counters.

"She's right about that being odd," Sunny agrees.

"Whatever. Alex doesn't mind, and it keeps things interesting."

Charlene says something, but I don't catch it.

They continue to debate the oddness of Violet's penchant for dressing up Alex's penis. I stay out of the conversation, because as much as I agree that it's strange, I've considered doing something similar to Randy. He's got a scar that makes his cock look like it's smiling when it's hard and frowning when it's soft.

We make one more stop about fifteen minutes from the cottage, partly because Sunny needs to pee again and also because we need groceries. With four hockey boys and a pregnant woman, there are a lot of food bases to cover in order to get through the weekend. Alex has already ordered a bunch of stuff that's scheduled to arrive tomorrow, but we still have dinner tonight, snacks, and possibly breakfast. Plus booze. The town we stop in is quaint, with cute little shops and a grocery store that caters to the rich people with cottages on Lake Geneva. The cottage is actually in Wisconsin, not Chicago, but it's just outside, so I call it the Chicago cottage to differentiate between this one and the one where Randy and I first met.

We pile out of the truck. Sunny stretches and groans, maybe because she gets stiff when she sits for too long. There's also a burger joint across the street. Sunny inhales deeply, and the groan becomes a sigh. Huh. Normally she'd be at least mildly grossed out. But now that I think about it, lately she's been suggesting stops at fast food places when we're out. Maybe it's so her vegan self can huff burgers without feeling guilty.

The boys get out of the SUV, and Darren finds the closest garbage can, tossing a few things into it. One of them looks very much like an empty bag of Doritos.

Charlene rushes over and looks in. "You didn't!"

A smile spreads across Darren's face. "I did." He wraps an arm around her waist, pulling her close. Charlene shrieks and tries to wrestle her way out of his grip, but Darren holds her ponytail so she can't move her head. He blows right in her face.

Charlene covers her mouth and nose with her palm while Darren laughs.

Randy gestures in their direction. "Someone should take a picture of that."

I pull out my phone and snap a bunch. "I assume that means he ate the Doritos."

"And a bag of Funyuns," Miller says.

I make a face. "Ew."

"Right?" Randy laces our fingers and pulls me toward the grocery store. "That's the most bizarre foreplay I've ever seen."

We leave them in the parking lot, grab a grocery cart, and divide and conquer the list. Randy and I spend a significant amount of time in the vegetable aisle. He manhandles all the dick-shaped produce while I take pictures, recording his silliness. When we come back out, we find Darren and Charlene in the back of the SUV. All the windows are open. He looks relaxed, based on the way his arm is stretched across the backseat. Charlene's face is red, and she looks tense. I'm not sure if the Doritos served their intended purpose or not.

We switch things up for the last leg of the trip, which is short. Sunny and Miller take the backseat of the truck, and Randy takes the wheel while I ride shotgun. We've all been to the Chicago cottage before—it was this past spring, right after Alex and Violet got married. They had a party to appease the moms, who didn't get to plan a wedding. Their Vegas wedding was exactly what those two needed, and not at all what Sunny's going to get when she and Miller tie the knot.

Skye, Violet's mom and Miller's stepmom, and Daisy, Sunny and Alex's mom, already have a list of three hundred guests, and it keeps growing. Sunny doesn't seem to mind, and neither does Miller. He's happy to have a set of moms who want to help out with things, since he lost his when he was a kid.

The only thing I'm worried about for this weekend is too much wedding talk. I've noticed that when we spend time with Miller and Sunny and wedding or baby talk comes up—which is frequently, all things considered—Randy gets quiet. I've assured him on more than one occasion that I'm not interested in getting knocked up, and he always laughs it off, but I think it makes him nervous anyway.

If I'm honest with myself, I'm not sure I ever want to get married. I don't necessarily believe it cements people together. Or makes them any more faithful to each other, which is Randy's primary hang up. I guess one of the good things about having no actual connection to my father is that there's nothing to miss, or deal with. Robbie Waters, Sunny and Alex's dad, has always been sort of a dad stand-in for me anyway.

We pull into the driveway behind Alex's SUV. Both of Alex's cottages are more house than cabin, but the one in Canada is far more rustic than this. This is a giant, modern house on a lake with lots of windows and gorgeous views of the water from every bedroom.

I love living in Chicago, but having grown up in the much quieter, more rural city of Guelph, the busy-ness of Chicago can be overwhelming. Coming up here, where we can relax and hang out and just be, is necessary sometimes. We unload all the groceries first, and then move upstairs to claim our rooms. The cottage has six bedrooms, all with connected bathrooms and private balconies. It's almost like staying at a bed and breakfast.

Randy follows me down the hall, away from Alex and Violet's bedroom. I've learned it's best to give those two some space. Violet is an excitable person, and that includes when she's getting her freak on. On more than one occasion we've overheard her declaring her love for Alex's monster cock.

Having accidentally seen Alex's unit once when we were growing up, I can say with definitive certainty that she's not exaggerating. Randy has a lot going on in that department, but I'm thankful he's not *that* big.

Once we're in our room, Randy closes the door, locking us in. "That was the longest two-hour drive ever."

I'm aware the quick-and-dirty sex we had in the changing room was a hold-over. Despite our mini discussion, I'm positive Randy's recent neediness is going to continue this weekend. He drops my suitcase and his duffle on the end of the bed, finds our toiletry bag, and inclines his head toward the bathroom.

"Interested in getting naked with me?"

"You want to shower before we go swimming?"

"Showering wasn't what I had in mind."

"Oh, no?"

He gives his head a slow shake.

"What kind of naked activity did you have in mind, then?"

"I was thinking more along the lines of a trip to the Vagina Emporium." He lifts his shirt over his head, exposing all those hard ridges and smooth planes of muscle.

"Is that so?"

Randy nods. "But first I want to make a pit stop at Boob Valley." He tugs the top of my dress so my breasts pop out. My nipples tighten in anticipation.

"And we can't do that right here? We need to be in the bathroom?" I arch as he circles my right nipple with a fingertip.

"No, but I was kinda hoping you wanted to watch me touch you." He leans in and kisses the swell of my breast, his soft beard rubbing my nipple.

I drop my face, using his hair to muffle my moan.

"And I don't want you to feel like you have to be all quiet." He sucks the tight peak, obviously trying to make a point.

I've come to learn part of Randy's thing with bathroom sex is because he's a fan of the mirror. He's not an egomaniac, but he likes to see what he's doing to me from an alternate perspective.

He holds out a hand, and I take it, excited for round one of cottage sex. I fully expect to be feeling it well into next week.

We're almost at the bathroom when someone starts pounding on our bedroom door.

Randy pulls me over the threshold. "Ignore it. They'll go away."

"Hey, guys, uh, Sunny has a bit of a problem," Miller says through the door.

Randy closes his eyes and exhales a long breath. "All I want is an all-access pass to the Vagina Emporium for an hour. Is that too damn much to ask?"

He sounds annoyed, but he pulls my dress back up to cover my boobs. Randy is nothing if not a loyal friend.

I kiss the side of his neck, close to his ear. "Tonight, when everyone goes to bed, you can have unlimited access."

"That's so fucking far away."

He's so cute when he's pouting.

I open the door to find Miller with his hands shoved in his pockets, looking distressed. He glances at Randy, who's shirtless, and then me. "I'm sorry I had to interrupt, but Sunny doesn't have a bathing suit top that fits."

Randy steps up behind me, ready to close the door in Miller's face. "You cockblocked me over a bathing suit top?"

"I know it sounds ridiculous, but—"

"Lily's bathing suit tops won't fit Sunny," Randy snaps.

I give him the eye. "Thanks for pointing that out."

"I'm not saying it to be a jerk. I fucking love your boobs, you know that." He goes to cup them, then realizes it's not a good time. "I'm pointing out that she's not going to get much coverage if she borrows something from you."

His argument is solid. "Violet should have something that will fit her."

"Uh, yeah, she's busy right now and, uh, Sunny's locked herself in the bathroom. She's crying, and I can't get her to stop." He looks to me. "I figured maybe you could help. I'm really sorry. I know the timing is shitty."

"Don't worry about it." I pat Randy on the chest. "Why don't you change into your bathing suit? I'll be back in a bit."

"If I cry, will you help me take care of my hard-on?" Randy asks. He's joking. Mostly.

"I'll manage your situation later." I leave him standing in the doorway, glaring at Miller as he and I walk away.

Sunny and Miller have taken the room next to us. From down the hall I can hear muffled, rhythmic thumping.

"Is that coming from Alex and Violet's room?" I ask.

"Pretty sure, yeah," Miller says, cringing.

"You'd think they'd pull the bed away from the wall."

"They might actually be having sex against the door."

"Right. Okay. That's not awkward."

"The story of my life, right there. I'm real sorry. I know everyone was probably looking for some private time, and I thought Sunny might be too, but then she got to unpacking..."

I give his shoulder a reassuring squeeze. "There's plenty of time for privacy later."

"I'm not sure Balls agrees with that."

"Randy wants what he wants when he wants it. And he usually gets it. It won't kill him to wait."

Miller ushers me into their room. Sunny's suitcase is open on the bed, a few items strewn on the comforter, but she's nowhere to be seen. I can hear her crying in the bathroom, though.

I knock and let her know it's me. She opens the door with a sniffle, one eye peeking through the narrow gap.

"Miller says you have bathing suit issues. Can I come in?"

She opens the door enough for me to get through. She has a team beach towel wrapped around her, hiding her bathing suit. Sunny is gorgeous in a modelesque way. I've always been envious of her long, curvy frame, which is so different from all my straight lines. Even though she's super pregnant, she still looks amazing. The only obvious change is the basketball-shaped bump rounding out her tummy—and how shiny and thick her hair is. Sunny's a walking advertisement for pregnancy. Not that it's working on me.

I'm more than happy to be an auntie for several years. I'd also settle for a dog, which is a lot like a child but without the same possibility for messing things up.

Sunny hiccups. "I can't go swimming this weekend."

As her due date approaches, her emotional state grows more unstable. I don't know if that's normal, or just because she's Sunny, but whatever the reason, she's been crying. A lot. And that's not the norm for Sunny. She's usually exactly like her name: full of positive energy.

"I'm sure it's not that bad."

Sunny drops the towel. She's wearing a pair of lemon yellow bikini bottoms; I recognize them from last summer. The top, which fit her perfectly then, doesn't cover even half of her chest.

"Wow. Your boobs have gotten a lot bigger."

"They're the size of my head."

"I wouldn't go quite that far."

"My nipples are gigantic, too. You can see them through the material! Miller liked my nipples before. What if they're always this big now? What if he doesn't like them anymore? What if he doesn't want to have sex with me this weekend? I'm so fat! And look at this line!" She points to her belly where a faint line runs from her navel and disappears under her bikini bottoms. "What is that even about? Why is it there?"

Sunny throws her arms around me, now in full-on sobbing mode. She's never been one to fixate on her physical appearance, so this insecurity is new.

"You're not fat, Sunny. You're pregnant, and you're gorgeous. We'll borrow a bathing suit top from Violet. I'm sure hers will fit you better."

I pat her back while she continues to cry. I have no idea if her nipples, which are very obvious through the bikini top, will ever go back to the way they were.

"What if I end up with stretch marks? Is it vain that I don't want stretch marks? I miss my body. I miss normal sex. I miss being able to see my feet and my vagina."

It's an epic breakdown. I'm not sure I've ever seen Sunny this upset, apart from when she and Miller were first dating and there were several unfortunate misunderstandings regarding pictures on social media.

I let her cry on me for another minute or two, and then Miller knocks on the door. "Sunny Sunshine? Can I do anything to help?"

"It's fine. I'm fine." Sunny hiccups at the end.

"You don't sound fine, sweets. Can you let me in? Please?"

"I don't want him to see me like this," Sunny whispers.

"Hasn't he seen you in a lot less than this recently?" I whisper back.

Sunny frowns as she ponders this. "Well, yes."

"So why are you worried about him seeing you in a bikini that's too small?"

Sunny twirls her hair around her finger and rubs it over her lips. It's what she does when she's thinking, and sometimes when she's nervous. She did it a lot when she and Miller were first dating and she wasn't sure she could handle being with someone who had such a terrible reputation with women. He's a reformed manwhore.

"I-I don't know?"

"So I can open the door for him?"

"I-I guess."

I flip the lock and open the door. Miller's arm is stretched over his head, holding the jamb.

He looks at me, and then at Sunny. His eyes go wide as he takes her in with a low whistle. "Wow." Miller raises his hands like he's cupping her chest. "Your boobs."

Sunny adjusts one of the cups; it doesn't make her boobs any less booby. "The top's too small."

Miller clears his throat. "Yeah. Just a little."

"I'll get a spare from Violet." I step around Miller, who's still holding his hands up like he's waiting for an oracle to drop into them. Or Sunny's boobs.

I pad down the hall to Violet and Alex's room and listen for a few seconds, crossing my fingers that they're done banging each other. There are no sexy sounds coming from inside, so I knock and wait.

Violet opens the door. Her long hair is pulled up in a messy ponytail. She's wearing a sheer, gauzy bathing suit cover-up over a red bikini. I'm immediately drawn to her cleavage. I can't even imagine how big her boobs are going to be when Alex knocks her up. And I assume that will happen sooner rather than later since Sunny's already started the trend and Alex likes to be first at everything.

"Hey! Wow. I didn't expect to see you for at least another hour or two," Violet says.

"We're not that bad."

She makes a face.

I don't defend myself further. I suppose Randy and I are usually that bad. When we went to Vegas a few months ago, Randy insisted we get our own suite so we didn't have to worry about getting called out on the amount of sex we have. If we still used condoms, I'd suggest we buy them in bulk.

I don't think there's anything wrong with having a healthy libido.

"I need to borrow a bikini top," I tell her.

Violet's eyes dart to my rack. "Umm..."

Six months ago I might've been offended. I used to be self-conscious about the size of my boobs, or the lack of size. But Randy loves them—he loves every part of me, actually—so I'm not nearly as hung up on how small they are anymore.

"It's not for me. It's for Sunny."

"Oh."

"She's busting out of her bikini and having a bit of a melt-down over it."

Alex appears in the doorway behind Violet. His hair is wet, like he just got out of the shower. "What's going on?"

"Sunny's boobs," Violet replies. "Hold on. I've got options." She brushes past Alex, who looks confused.

"Do I even want an explanation?" he asks.

"Sunny's boobs are preparing to be feedbags," Violet calls from the bedroom.

"Oh. Right. Okay. I'll meet you girls down at the dock then." He steps around me, as if he can't get out of here fast enough.

Violet rummages through her dresser, slinging bathing suit tops over her shoulder.

"Wow. How many bikinis do you have?"

"A lot." She holds another one up, shakes her head, and tosses it on the dresser. "You know how some guys buy lots of baseball caps and some women have shoe and purse fetishes?"

"Sure. I guess." I'm not sure what this has to do with the ridiculous number of bathing suits Violet owns, but often her conversation starters don't make a lot of sense.

"Alex has a bikini fetish. He buys them for me all the time. Actually, he buys them for my boobs. I think he gift wraps them so he can address the cards to my boobs."

"You two are crazy, you know that?"

"Oh yeah, totally." She shoves the drawer closed with her hip, and I follow her down the hall. "I have bathing suit options!" Violet announces as we step into Sunny and Miller's room.

The door is wide open, so that should be a sure sign it's safe to enter. It isn't.

Sunny's sitting on the bathroom vanity, with Miller standing between her legs. His bathing suit shorts are pushed down so half of his Day-Glo white ass is showing. She's got one hand in his hair, and the other is grabbing a handful of ass cheek. They very well may be having sex, based on the way they're moving against each other.

"Goddamn it! Are you boning? Why the hell is the door open? Your yeti ass is blinding me!" Violet throws the bikinis up in the air and spins around. "Just you wait, Buck! I'm going to get you back for this, and I promise it's going to be a million times worse than your hairy bare ass," Violet yells as she walks out of the room.

"I'll come back later!" I pull the door closed behind me.

Violet huffs. "I need a damn drink."

"I need to bleach my brain."

"I'll see you down at the dock." Violet grumbles to herself about therapy and yetis as she disappears downstairs.

I can feel the flush in my cheeks as I hurry down the hall away from Miller and Sunny's room. I'd prefer not to hear Sunny's moans of pleasure if I can avoid it. I fully expect Randy to be down at the dock already, having given up on getting into the Vagina Emporium, so I'm surprised to find him lying on the bed when I enter our room.

He's wearing his swim shorts, but they're undone and his cock is peeking out of the waistband. He's hard. There's a note-card sitting on his chest. This should be interesting.

I close the door and lock it, then tiptoe over to the bed. He could be asleep. It's not unusual for him to be sporting wood and unconscious. I lean in and whisper, "Raaaandy," close to his ear. I get nothing. Not even a flinch.

I pluck the note from his chest and giggle at the block letters written across the top in Randy's rushed scrawl. It reads:

RIP

Randall Ballistic

COD: lack of access to Lily's

Vagina Emporium

To revive me, you can try the

following (remember to start

with step one):

1. Sit on my face

2. Kiss moody dick

(full-mouth hugs are always

welcome)

3. If steps one and two fail,

give moody dick an all-access

pass to the Vagina Emporium

I toss the card on his chest with a snort and take a step toward the bathroom.

Randy latches onto my wrist. "Where do you think you're going?"

I stumble and drop down on the bed. His eyes are still closed. "I thought you were resting in peace."

I get no response this time, just a tiny tic in his left cheek. He releases my wrist and goes back to playing dead. I have no idea what to expect. I assume using the bathroom to freshen up is out of the question, though. I also don't think we'll be making it to the dock prior to him getting inside me.

I take off my dress and panties, leaving them in a pile on the floor. Climbing up onto the mattress, I kneel beside him. I take a few moments to appreciate how beautiful he is. I don't know how I managed to make this man mine, but I love him in an intensely consuming way. I run my hand down his chest. When I get to his navel, he stops my hand.

He cracks a lid. "Step one." He closes his eye again and releases my hand.

"You know, you're pretty demanding for someone who's supposed to be dead."

His mouth twitches, but he remains still otherwise. He's in a funny mood today. I'm interested to see how the rest of the weekend plays out. I circle the head of his cock with a fingertip, then bend down to give it a quick kiss before I move into position on his chest.

I run my fingers through his hair and trace the arch of his eyebrows, admiring him for a few seconds because I don't always have the chance. As I've mentioned, Randy doesn't usually like to wait for what he wants. This notecard approach is something new. I lean forward and kiss the end of his nose. He tilts his head back. I can see a hint of his honey eyes through the slit in his lids.

He cups the back of my head, and his tongue darts out to lick my mouth. "Wrong set of lips, luscious."

"You're impatient today, aren't you?"

"You would be too if you had to wait all damn day to get inside your girlfriend."

"All damn day? You've finger-fucked me, tongue-fucked me, and pussy-fucked me all in the last five hours."

"All of that was too rushed to count. Now get your ass up here and get on my face."

I shriek when he slaps my behind. Losing my balance, I topple forward, allowing Randy to move me into position. He shifts me so my knees are on either side of his head. Running his hands up my legs, he grabs my ass and pulls me down over his mouth.

"Oh, God," I groan as he licks from my entrance to my clit, then drops his head back on the bed. His smile tells me he thinks he's won whatever game he's playing.

He kisses the inside of my thigh. "How many times you think I can make you come like this, eh, luscious?"

"Hmm." I tap my lip thoughtfully. "Maybe once or twice?"

Randy makes a disbelieving sound. "I'm gonna say at least four."

"Pretty full of yourself, aren't you?"

He bites the juncture of my thigh, his beard rubbing sensitive skin. "Pretty soon you're gonna be begging to be full of me."

"Oh, you think so, do you?"

"I know so." He's so cocky.

He lifts his head like he's going for my clit. Before he can latch on and start sucking, I plant a palm on his forehead and pin his head to the mattress.

"You don't want me to eat you?"

I sure as hell do. Randy usually leads in the bedroom. I don't have an issue with that. After seven years with an apathetic lover, it's amazing to have someone who wants to make me feel good all the time. It's Randy's personal life mission to outdo every orgasm with an even better one the next time. But sometimes I like to change it up, like now.

I want to capitalize on his current playfulness since this week has been tense. I sweep my fingertips over his lips. When he tries to nip them, I snatch them away, bringing them to my own mouth. I still have a hand on his forehead. He's more than capable of removing it and taking what he wants, but I think he's as intrigued to see what I'm going to do as I am.

I bite my knuckle then suck on my finger, swirling my tongue around the tip, like I would if it were his cock. The hand on the back of my thigh tightens as I drag my finger down my chin and over my throat. I veer left and circle my nipple on the descent, rolling it between my fingers.

"Lily." It sounds like a warning.

"Randy." It's almost a moan.

He starts to lift his head.

"Not yet, baby," I murmur.

"Not yet? What the fuck do you want me to wait for?"

I grin as I circle my navel and dip lower. I sigh as I skim my clit. I'm hovering about six inches above Randy's face. I know I'm driving him insane. His hot stare is fixed on where I'm touching myself as I slide a single finger inside. I ease out and circle my clit, repeating the circuit a few more times.

"Want this?" I ask, holding the finger that was inside me two inches above Randy's lips.

"Give it," he growls.

"Mmm, on second thought—" I snatch it away, but Randy's fast. He grabs for my hand, so I react instinctively and jam it in my own mouth—not my whole hand, just the finger.

"Fucking Christ, Lily." He squeezes my ass, and I have to hold on to the headboard so I don't lose my balance again. There's no warm-up. He flat-tongues my clit, then seals his mouth around it, sucking hard.

I cry out because the sensation is everything I expect it to be. When I'm not at risk of falling over anymore, I lean back and thread my fingers through Randy's hair. His nose is mashed against my pelvis. I'm not sure how he's managing to breathe, considering the way he's devouring me, but he hasn't passed out from lack of oxygen yet, so I'll put the worry on hold.

After the first orgasm, he detaches from my clit and holds up a finger. "That's one." And just like earlier today, there's no reprieve. He reattaches and starts sucking again. The second orgasm comes fast and hard. "Two."

He changes it up after that, lapping at me with slow strokes that might not have the same effect if I hadn't already come twice. I shake my head as a third orgasm washes over me and notice the door to the bathroom is open. From here I have an amazing view of me straddling Randy's face in the mirror. He's holding my ass, fingers digging in as he rocks me over his mouth. His cock is hard, pushing against his swim shorts and more than half exposed now, just waiting for me to ride it. Which I'm ready to do, but Randy's still eating, and when he has an orgasm goal, he won't stop until he reaches it.

"You getting bored, luscious?" He nibbles at my non-face lips.

"What? No." I glance back at him.

"Whatcha looking at?"

"You eating me out in the bathroom mirror."

"Oh yeah?" And suddenly I'm airborne.

I land on my back on the bed. Randy checks out my previous view, then decides the bathroom mirror is too far away and the one over the dresser provides a much better, much closer view of events.

He kicks off his swim shorts, his erection jutting out. At first I don't quite get what his plan is as he lays me on my side and checks the view in the mirror. He positions himself behind me, kisses my hip, and trails a finger along the outside of my thigh. Then he lifts my leg and ducks under, his gaze on the mirror across the room as he kisses a trail down the inside of my thigh. I giggle at the tickle of his beard, and moan when he licks me again, soft and slow.

"You should use your fingers this time," I suggest.

"Should I now?"

"Uh-huh," I half moan as he circles my clit with the tip of his tongue.

"My tongue isn't good enough for you?"

"I love your tongue. It's amazing. I'm just saying, fingers are great, too." Randy rarely adds digits to the eating equation. I used to think it was because he finds the multitasking distracting. That has nothing to do with it.

He hums against me, and I feel his thumbs or fingers near where I asked for them, but he doesn't follow through. Instead he goes back to devouring me. He has to hold my hips with both hands to stop me from thrashing around and potentially kicking him in the face. When orgasm number four body-slams me, he shifts so he can run the head of his cock over my hypersensitive clit.

"I should suck cock," I mumble, making a half-assed attempt to sit up.

Randy snickers. "You can do that later."

He props my leg up on his shoulder and holds the other one open, observing his actions in the mirror for a few seconds as he continues to rub his tip around and around my clit. He goes lower and circles the Vagina Emporium entrance, but he doesn't make a move to get in there. Tease.

"How you feeling?" he asks.

"Ready for cock." It comes out raspy, probably from all my moaning and coming.

"Is that right?"

"Mmm." I lift my hips, hoping to encourage him to go ahead and give it to me, like I'm sure he wants to.

He taps my clit, causing me to jerk. His grin is downright evil. "How bad do you want it?"

I can't believe he's still holding out. Usually after an epic lick-off, Randy doesn't take any time putting his dick where he wants it, or where I do. "On a scale of one to ten?"

"Sure. That works."

I should be sated after four orgasms. But I'm not, and I think I've figured out why: often when Randy eats me out, he uses *only* tongue. And while I may come like a machine, the lack of fingering makes them somehow unsatisfying. It's like my vagina is aware there's something missing. And Randy must have figured it out, too. So I have to assume he's done it on purpose—and then I remember him saying I'd be begging to be full of him. Damn it. He's so not winning this game of his. He should already feel like he's won with the four orgasms.

I bite my lip and go for the innocent look. "Mmm, about a five."

His eyes narrow. "Five?"

"Okay, how about a six?"

He pushes my leg off his shoulder and sits back on his heels. He's holding his cock in his fist, thumb sweeping back and forth over the tip. "Maybe I should take this to the bathroom and finish myself off in there if you're that uninterested." He sounds frighteningly serious, and he's got one foot on the floor.

"What? No." I scramble to my knees and wrap my arms around his neck. His erection pokes my stomach. "One hundred. On a scale of one to ten, I'm at one hundred."

"I don't know if I believe you." He's still fisting his cock; his knuckles rub my pelvis.

I press my chest against his. "I thought we were playing."

"So now that you think I'm gonna take away your fun, you decide you want me?"

I shake my head.

"No? You don't want me?"

"I *need* you that bad."

This gets a smile out of him. My man needs to be needed these days. I don't have a problem with that, as long as I understand where the insecurity is coming from. Which I think I do.

I pull him back on the bed, and he settles between my legs. I don't rush him this time. Instead, I let him tease me, and eventually I do exactly what he said I would: I beg to have him inside me.

When I'm on the verge of coming, he props himself up on one arm and splays his other hand across my sternum. His eyes stay on me as he moves, hips rocking slowly, so different from the eating-orgasm marathon.

I cup his cheek and pull him closer. "I love you," I whisper against his lips.

"I love you back."

He kisses me when I come, swallowing his name.

BEARD CONDITIONING

RANDY

I lie on top of Lily for a few minutes after I come. Not because I can't move, but because I don't want to. I know I'm being needy and weird, but there's a lot going on right now, and I'm feeling anxious. Also, if I move from this spot, there's a good chance I'll make a mess all over the comforter, and this isn't my cottage or my bed. There are laundry facilities, but it's not like it won't be obvious what was going down if we have to wash the quilt an hour after arriving.

After another minute or two of me being Lily's human blanket, she says softly, "We should probably go down to the dock and be social for a few hours."

"Probably," I agree.

She pats my ass. "Let me up so I can put a bathing suit on."

I tuck an arm underneath her and roll us over, then shimmy until we're at the edge of the bed.

"What're you doing?"

"Not making a mess on the comforter."

"Oh. Good call. We should get a plastic sheet for the rest of the weekend."

I spin us around until I can plant my feet on the ground. Then I stand, with Lily still attached to me, and walk us to the bathroom. My dick is still half-hard. I could totally go again, but I realize we've been up here for a while, and round two is always longer than round one. We've been missing long enough.

When we're in front of the vanity, I turn on the tap. I hold on to her ass, lift her off my cock, and position her over the sink.

"We have way too much practice with this move," Lily observes, her arms still wrapped around my neck.

I bounce her around a bit before I set her down. "Yeah, but we don't have to change sheets as often this way."

She kisses my chest, and I drop my head so I can get a real one. She gives me her cheek. "Oooh. You need to wash that beard."

I check out my reflection. "Jesus. You made a mess."

Lily tweaks my nipple. "Jerk!"

"I love it when you condition my beard."

She makes a gagging sound. "You're so classy."

I bite her finger. Then I bring it up to my nose and take a sniff. It's the one she wouldn't give me when she was playing with me—and herself.

She tries to pull it out of my grasp. "What're you doing?"

I slide my free fingers into the hair at the nape of her neck and bring hers to her nose. "You should probably wash your hands."

She shoves my hand away. "Oh my God! You're so gross!"

I link my fingers with hers. "Do you have any idea how fucking hot that was?"

"How hot what was?"

I'm still holding on to her hair, so when I run my nose along her cheek, she can't get away from me.

"Finger-fucking yourself two inches above my face. The view was extraordinary."

"Oh. I thought you might like that." Her voice is soft, breathy.

"I liked it a lot." I nip at her jaw. "You know what else I liked?"

"What else did you like?" I can barely hear her now.

We may not make it out of this room before dinner; it may be tomorrow morning. "Guess."

"I'm not good at guessing games."

"Come on, Lily. Or are you feeling all shy now?" I back up so I can see her face.

Her cheeks are flushed. Her eyes dart away. After all the sex we have, in all the locations, nothing should embarrass her, but clearly this does, which is why I'm pushing for an answer. And also, it's fucking hot. I want her to do it again, only next time I want to be in on the action.

She lifts her eyes, and her cheeks grow even pinker. It's barely a whisper when she asks, "Did you like it when I tasted myself?"

"So fucking much. You have no idea." I pull her forward and rub my now full-on hard-on against her.

Lily's eyes roll up. "I have a pretty decent idea. You know, in case you were worried, I have no interest in eating pussy; I'm totally a moody dick fan."

"Thanks for the reassurance. You know I was a little concerned, especially with how worked up you get when I kiss you after I've gone down."

"What?"

"It's okay, Lily Pad."

"Was I unclear when Violet tried that? That's not a nickname you're allowed to start using."

"You don't like it? I think it's cute."

"Cute? Now I really don't like it."

"Fine. I was just trying it out, luscious. And getting off on your taste in my mouth is nothing to be ashamed of. It's cool if you went through an experimental phase in college. I don't even mind if you want to tell me about it." I'm fucking with her, mostly because I'm one-thousand percent sure she *didn't* have an experimental phase. Or if she did, it didn't include dining from the girl buffet.

She bites her lip and gives me a shy smile. "Well, there was this one time freshman year when I stayed overnight in the all-girls dorm…"

"What?"

She snorts. "Oh my God, your face right now."

"Are you serious?"

"No. I'm not serious, but if you want me to make up a story, I'm happy to do that for you."

"I'm good with your pussy being the only one you taste, like, ever."

"Kinda like I'm good with being the only one who ever made you come from a blow job."

"Exactly."

Yeah, we're not leaving this room for a while.

It's another half hour before we exit the bathroom. When I'm done with Lily, she's had two more orgasms, and she's promised me a blow job later, after we spend some time at the dock.

She picks up the foaming soap pump and squirts it on my half-limp dick, then looks at the label. "Oh, moody dick is going to smell like black cherry merlot. Fancy."

"You like red wine, right?" Some of the foam drips onto the floor.

"I do. He'll be a tasty treat later." She hops off the vanity. "You want help with that."

"It's probably better if I take care of this on my own. Why don't you put one of your new bathing suits on for me?"

53

She pauses to watch me lather up my cock. "You mean the one you bought me last week?"

"What are you talking about? I didn't buy you a new one."

"Liar." She pinches my ass. "Just because you take the tags off and hide it in my drawer doesn't mean I don't notice it's new." She wraps her arms around me from behind and kisses between my shoulder blades. "But thank you for your devious generosity."

"It's highly self-serving. I like imagining the ways I can remove those suits when we're alone."

Lily chuckles and disappears into the bedroom while I finish cleaning my dick and go to work on rinsing her out of my beard. I'm finishing up when she walks back into the bathroom wearing her newest bikini. The one I "didn't" buy for her.

She twirls around. "What do you think?"

I let out a low whistle. The top is one of those things with no straps, which she can pull off, and the bottoms look like a little skirt. It reminds me of one of her skating outfits, except with way less material. It's white, and Lily has naturally tanned skin that darkens in the summer. Like now.

She flicks the ruffle at her ass. "You did a good job."

"Maybe a little too good."

She beams; it's the perfect reaction. Lily spent a long time with a boyfriend who didn't appreciate how gorgeous her body is. She's finally starting to own it, which is awesome. I want her to feel beautiful, because she is.

I put on my swim shorts and grab our towels while Lily throws sunglasses, sunscreen, and a bunch of other crap in an oversized bag. We make a pit stop in the kitchen for snacks and drinks. I picked up wine coolers for Lily because she's a lightweight when it comes to booze. She shouldn't get sloppy drunk if I dole them out slowly. Though I'm not sure how successful I'll be—Violet and Charlene like to tie one on, and they often coerce Lily into doing the same. Maybe since Sunny's not drinking they'll tone it down.

It's after five, but the sun is still hitting the dock. We have a few hours before we lose the heat and the light. And we have all day tomorrow and Sunday to relax and enjoy the end of summer. Soon we'll be back in training camp, so I want to enjoy what's left of the off-season.

Hockey season means being on the road half the time, and that'll be an adjustment. It's a good thing I have teammates in the same position, missing their women too. Sometimes I still worry that I'm too much like my dad, and I'm going to fuck up this good thing by doing something regrettable. His recent phone calls have reminded me of this possibility and ramped up my anxiety over the coming changes.

I follow Lily outside, my eyes on her ass and that flouncy little skirt bottom. We're definitely going to have sex while she's wearing that. I'm already planning out the video since I'm stockpiling for away games. We need a mirror for this one. I shake my head and shut down those thoughts because a hard-on in swim shorts is difficult to hide. And this weekend can't be *just* about sex.

The guys are set up in a semicircle on the dock, facing the water and the sun. Sunny's reclined in a lounger with her feet in Miller's lap. He's painting her toenails.

The dogs are lying next to her. Wiener jumps and barks as we approach, then hides behind Sunny's chair.

"Looking to start a new career?" I ask Miller as I drop our towels on an empty chair.

He finishes the toe he's working on before he flips me the bird. "Keep your comments to yourself, Balls."

Lily sighs. "That is so sweet!"

Sunny flips up her sunglasses and gives Miller a warm smile. "He's so good to me." She pats her basketball belly. "This makes doing my toes so awkward, and Miller does a nice job."

"Anything for you, sweets."

"Look who decided to take a boning break!" Violet calls.

55

She and Charlene are relaxing in the lake on floating lounge chairs, secured to the dock with a tow rope.

"Who says we were boning? Maybe we were having a nap," I call back.

"Based on all the moaning, I'd say that's a load of balls." She pulls one of her hip thrusts. It makes her chair rock in the water. She holds on to the armrests as her drink sloshes over the side.

"Ha ha. You're so funny." Lily's cheeks flush pink.

"Um." Sunny adjusts her wide-brimmed hat. "Actually, your windows were open, so…"

"Oh, God." Lily turns her face into my chest.

"We turned on some music. It pretty much drowned everything out," Alex reassures her.

"I'm sorry." She bites me. "This is your fault."

"Don't be sorry. It's good to know Ballistic is taking care of you." Darren doesn't crack a smile, so I can't tell if he's actually serious.

Alex elbows him in the arm as he tips back his beer, so it dribbles down his chest.

"What?" He wipes away the wet spot with a shirt and looks over at Charlene, who's busy adjusting Violet's bikini top so she doesn't accidentally flash anyone. "You gotta take care of what's yours if you want to keep it."

That's a weird way to word it, even though I understand what he means.

"When Sunny's done with her pedicure, you two should come join us in the water!" Charlene says to the girls.

I kiss Lily's shoulder. "We should put some sunscreen on you before you do that."

"Good idea. I'll do you if you do me."

"I thought we were gonna hang out down here for a while."

She tweaks my nipple, and I wrap an arm around her, pinning her arms to her side. She shrieks as I drop down into an empty chair.

56

"For the love of broken beavers, do you two ever take a break? Seriously. Is your vagina lined with leather?" Violet asks.

"Envious of my pussy powers?" Lily shoots back.

"I honestly wouldn't be surprised if one day your vagina fell right off. Dropped right out of your little skating skirt," Violet replies.

"Then it would be a pocket pussy!" Charlene interjects.

"Can we reserve the pocket pussy conversations for later, when half the lake can't hear you?" Alex nods in the direction of the neighboring dock, where a bunch of teenagers are hanging out.

Violet grimaces, but stops with the pussy parlay.

Lily works on her legs while I rub suntan lotion into her back. I also help get the back of her legs, adjusting the ass of her bikini so she's not flashing cheek. She smacks my hand when I get too close to her pussy. "I'm being thorough."

"You're being a perv."

"A thorough perv."

By the time Lily's done my back, Miller has finished painting Sunny's toes. Lily ties two more of the floating lounge chairs to the dock. Miller helps Sunny into her lounger, making sure she's balanced before he sits back down.

"Either of you hear from Lance today?" Alex asks.

"He had something he had to take care. He was real vague about it," Miller says.

When Lance Romero, another one of our teammates, is vague about his plans, it usually doesn't mean good things. "You think it's Tash-related?" I ask.

"Probably."

A while back when Alex and Violet threw a "little" party, Tash was invited. Lance said he was okay with it, but I have a feeling seeing her didn't do him any favors. They were involved last season, which ended up being a huge clusterfuck. She was our team trainer and lost her job over it. Anyway, they disappeared together at the end of the night, and Lance wouldn't answer calls the next day. We ended up stopping by his place to make sure he was okay. He wasn't. It took a couple of days to clean up the mess, and him.

Alex taps the arm of his chair. "I'll get Vi to message him in a bit."

"Why Vi?" I ask.

"He talks to her. She might be able to convince him to come up here for a couple of days instead of dealing with it alone."

"What do you mean he talks to her?"

"Like, about personal stuff. I don't know. I don't get into it."

"And you're okay with that?" Lance is my friend, but he makes some questionable choices.

Alex nods. "What he tells her in confidence isn't my business. He's a good guy. He was a big help to Violet after I had that concussion earlier this year. He's loyal; I don't think he's had the easiest life."

Lance doesn't talk about his family, other than to make the occasional passing comment about having to see them on holidays.

"Family can fuck you up," Darren says.

Violet calls for another drink, and Alex suggests she take a break if she wants to make it past eight o'clock. When it's clear he's not moving, she decides to get it herself and paddles her chair over to the edge of the dock.

"Any bets on Vi falling in?"

Darren raises a finger. "I'll put twenty on that."

"She's not that drunk," Alex grumbles.

"Maybe not, but she's that uncoordinated." Miller roots around in the bag beside him and pulls out his phone. "I'mma record this, just in case I'm right."

"So you're putting money on her making it to the dock without going under first?" I look at Alex, but he's not paying attention to me. He's focused on Violet.

She's clearly calculating how to get her ass from the floating chair to the edge of the dock.

"Baby, why don't you go around to the ladder?" Alex stands, like he's about to help her.

Instead she hoofs one leg up. She's about halfway there when Miller shouts, "Hey! Isn't that a dock spider?"

Violet shrieks and starts flailing. Alex rushes to help her, but he doesn't make it before her chair tips, and she goes under. She comes up splashing and screaming. "Get it off! Where is it? Those fuckers swim!"

"Please tell me you're getting this," I say to Miller.

"Oh yeah, it's epic."

Instead of taking Alex's offered hand, Violet grabs Charlene's chair and tries to climb, tipping it over, too.

Darren barks out a laugh as she comes bobbing to the surface.

I shove my hand in the bag Lily brought down, searching for a phone. I come up empty-handed, which is unfortunate, because the look on Lily's face is priceless.

I'll get Miller to send me the video so I can pull a few still shots.

"Baby, there's no spider. Miller was being a dick. C'mere." Alex shoots the bird over his shoulder, then crouches down and grabs Violet under the arms, hoisting her out of the water. She wraps her arms around his neck and her legs around his waist. She's still freaking out, swatting at her back while Alex tries not to get hit in the face. "Calm down, Violet."

"Someone owes me twenty," Darren says.

Sunny points a disapproving finger at Miller. "No cookie for you tonight."

Miller's smile drops, and he stops filming. "Come on, sweets; it was funny."

Violet pushes away from Alex when she finally realizes she's not being attacked by a spider. "You asshole!" she yells, stomping toward Miller. "Did you take pictures of that? Gimme your phone, you yeti bastard! As if the ass-blinding earlier wasn't bad enough!" She reaches for it, but Miller raises it over his head, laughing.

Darren and Alex are communicating with hand gestures. He gets out of his chair and moves to stand behind Miller. Snatching the phone out of Miller's hand, Darren tosses it to me. I almost fumble it, but manage to recover. He and Alex each seize an arm and drag Miller across the dock, heaving him over the side. The splash soaks Sunny and Lily, who had managed to remain fairly dry up to this point. Their shocked cries turn to outrage when Darren pushes Alex in. I return the favor by pushing Darren off the dock, and then cannonball right beside Lily.

When I pop up beside her, she dunks my head back under. I retaliate by swimming beneath her chair and flipping her over. She comes up sputtering. She wraps herself around me and grabs hold of her overturned floaty chair so she doesn't drag us underwater. She's dense muscle and low body fat, so regardless of how little she weighs, she's like human lead.

We spend the next hour in the water, during which I constantly try to get my hand into her bikini bottoms. After a while Lily's lips start to turn blue. Being as lean as she is, she gets cold fast. We get out of the water before everyone else. I wrap her in a towel and cuddle with her in a chair.

By seven thirty, the sun is starting to dip below the tree line, and we're all hungry, so we pack up and return to the cottage to get changed and start dinner.

I grab Lily around the waist as soon as we're in the room, reaching behind me to flip the lock.

"Oh, no. No way. We're not doing this right now. I'm starving, and I said I'd help with dinner."

"Just a quickie." I pull the top of her bathing suit down so her breasts pop out. She breaks out in a wave of goosebumps. Her nipples are already hard.

"There's no such thing as a quickie with you, and you know it." She presses her ass back against my hard-on.

"Everyone's having showers, and you're freezing. Let me warm you up." I kiss along her shoulder. "I wanna make a video

60

of you in this bikini. I've been thinking about fucking you in it all afternoon."

Mainly I want the videos for away games. Lily's the only person I've ever done anything like that with, and I like them even more for that reason. I mean yeah, lots of bunnies happily sent me unrequested naked pictures, but it's different with Lily. I think it's similar to my current obsession with mirrors. I'm hooked on the raw emotion and vulnerability Lily shows in those moments.

"We can make a video later."

"Just a couple of pictures, then?" I slide my hand down the front of her bikini bottoms. "You need to see how this looks from my vantage point."

She makes a plaintive sound when I brush over her clit. "Okay. A few pictures."

I withdraw my hand and give her ass a tap. "Awesome. Why don't you turn on the water, and I'll get my phone."

She doesn't pull the top back up, just runs on her tiptoes to the bathroom. I check my shorts for my phone, but it's not in there, so I check the comforter and under the bed.

Lily peeks her head out. "What's taking so long?"

"I'm looking for my phone."

"You probably left it in the truck. Mine's in my purse."

I nab her purse from the floor and bring it to her, because I'm not going through that. I have no idea what kind of stuff she carries around in there. Once she finds her phone, she keys in her code and passes it to me.

I put my hand down the front of her bikini bottoms again and snap a few pictures, then show them to her. "See how hot that is?"

"I see." She tilts her head to the side so I have more places to kiss.

I take a few more pictures like that before I bend her over and take a few of her sweet ass. Sliding my finger under the elastic, I pull the fabric to the side, exposing her cheek. Lily spreads her legs for me, and I snap a few more shots, capturing frame by frame as I ease a finger inside her.

"Wanna see?" I ask.

At her nod, I scroll back and flip through them for her—while I'm finger-fucking her. She moans her discontent when I stop.

"Don't worry, luscious, you'll get what you want." I use the head of my cock to nudge the fabric out of the way. Then I hit record as the head disappears inside her. I transfer the phone to my other hand and hold the fabric out of the way so I can watch the first thrust.

"How's the view?" Lily asks.

"Amazing." I hit pause, then rewind it, holding it out in front of us for her to see while I fuck her slow. "So much better than internet porn."

Lily takes the phone, and I start fucking her like I mean it. She stays as steady as she can, holding the phone up in the mirror, her eyes on the tiny image on the screen. She zeros in on my hand as I move her bikini bottoms to the side and rub her clit. When she's too shaky, she drops the phone on the counter and grabs the back of my neck, seeking my mouth.

She comes first, then drops to her knees. I pick up the phone again and record her as she licks herself off my cock and sucks me until I come, too. Usually I'm careful when I'm recording and don't get her face, but that's pretty unavoidable when a blow job is involved.

She brushes her teeth as soon as we're done and then joins me in the shower. "Don't let me forget to delete that from my phone as soon as we're home and I've downloaded it to my laptop," she tells me.

"Good plan."

5

SERIOUSLY. WHAT'S HAPPENING HERE?

LILY

We're quick about the shower since the "photo shoot" took longer than planned. I pull on a pair of leggings, a bandeau bra, and one of the new tops Randy recently bought and hid in my drawer. It's pale pink and has little brown wiener dogs all over it.

He thinks he's being all smooth; he takes off the tags and folds the new stuff up like it was there all along. I love how thoughtful he is, and I know I'm important to him in ways no one else is. He cleared out one entire side of his dresser and closet to make room for my things. I didn't have a lot to begin with, but he keeps filling up the space with things he thinks I'll like or need. It's sweet.

By the time we make it to the kitchen, dinner preparations

are in full swing. I get a knife and start chopping vegetables. Randy takes the foil-wrapped double-stuffed potatoes outside to the barbecue.

"So Lily, important question for you." Violet's peeling carrots at crotch level. It's a little disturbing.

"Shoot."

She sets down her peeler, looking rather serious. "How do you keep your vag from chafing with the amount of dick you take from Balls?"

"Paraffin wax baths," I reply evenly. "Hey, where's Sunny?"

"She's outside with Miller, watching him barbecue."

Charlene looks over at me. She's wearing a pair of latex gloves while chopping onions. "Doesn't she usually get squicked out by meat?"

"Usually. I mean, at the beginning of her pregnancy, if she even passed a burger joint she'd be heaving, but lately she's been sniffing my Epic Burger bags."

Darren passes through the kitchen and stops behind Charlene. "You ladies need help with anything in here?"

Charlene's hand flutters to her throat, and panic flares across her face.

He retrieves the necklace she's always wearing from his pocket. Hanging it from a finger, he holds it up in front of her. "Missing something, dollface?"

"Oh my God." She grabs for it, but he snatches it away. "Where did you find it?"

"In your beach bag."

"I didn't want to lose it."

"Of course not." He moves her hair over her shoulder. "Let me put it back on for you."

She drops her chin, bowing her head as he clasps it behind her neck and follows with a soft kiss at the top of her spine. Charlene shivers, and I get busy with the lettuce. I feel like an interloper on a very private moment.

Charlene startles me when she blurts out, "No!"

Her knife clatters to the counter, and she latches onto Darren's wrist with both hands.

"No?" He cocks a brow. They're rather villainous and archy.

Her eyes are wide. "No. They're raw. Please."

It takes me a second to realize she's talking about the onions. An amused grin plays over his mouth, but he drops the rings back on the chopping board. "Why don't you help me bring the beers out?"

Charlene heaves a relieved sigh, peels off her gloves, and takes two bottles, passing the others to Darren. He links the fingers of his free hand through hers, and she follows him through the screen door on to the deck.

Violet and I make eye contact.

"Okay. Is it just me, or was that really fucking weird?"

"That was really fucking weird," Violet agrees.

"What the hell is going on with those two?"

"Honestly, I have no idea, but this stinky food business is starting to freak me out. We need to get her hammered and make her talk."

"Yes. I'll make some margaritas. They're like truth serum."

"This is why we're soul sisters, right there—that and we both have men with giant dicks."

I raise my hand for a high five as I pass. She shoves it out of the way and forces me to do a chest bump instead.

Once the veggies are prepared and I've made a pitcher of margaritas, plus a non-alcoholic one for Sunny, we take everything outside and join the rest of them on the deck. It's still warm, although the sun has sunk below the tree line now. Pretty decorative lights wrap around the deck railing, illuminating the space. In addition to a huge dining table inside, there's also a screened-in porch, complete with a chandelier and seating for ten. It overlooks the water, and it's the perfect setting for dinner.

Sunny's currently hanging off of Miller's arm while he flips steaks. Darren and Charlene magically appear again fifteen minutes before dinner. They both seem composed, if not tense, which makes me even more curious about what the heck the onion-Doritos thing is.

Sunny practically sits in Miller's lap during dinner. I think she's sniffing his shirt. If she wasn't pregnant, I'd wonder if she was high.

"Charlene, I've been meaning to ask where you got your necklace. It's so pretty." I try to be nonchalant about it, but based on Violet's glare, it's way obvious what I'm up to. Also, I've had two margaritas and a lot of sun today, so I'm feeling the booze even with the steak-and-potatoes buffer.

Charlene fingers the pearls. "Oh, uh, it was a gift."

"You must love it since you wear it all the time," Sunny chimes in.

She's still all snuggled up to Miller, making it a challenge for him to eat. He's resorted to stabbing his steak and biting off hunks since he doesn't have a free hand to cut it with.

I nod in agreement. "You hardly ever take it off."

"Pearls are Charlene's favorite." Darren traces the edge of the necklace with a fingertip. "Isn't that right?"

Charlene blinks several times, rapidly. Now, she and Violet are probably the most open people I've ever met when it comes to discussing sexual adventures. So I'm surprised by the flush that creeps into her cheeks. She puts her hand over Darren's when he slips a finger under the necklace.

"I love pearls." She's almost breathless.

This is so weird.

"It's a symbol of Darren's favorite spot to unload," Violet says, breaking the sexual tension. I'd like to say it's because she's as drunk as I am, but she's not.

Darren snorts and whispers something to Charlene, who chokes on her margarita.

Before I can segue to asking about the Doritos and raw onions diet they're on, a flash of headlights and the sound of throbbing bass freeze us all in place. The lights and noise cease just as abruptly.

Violet checks her phone. "Oh, shit. I missed a few messages. It looks like Lance decided to come after all."

Less than a minute later, Lance comes around the side of the deck with a duffle bag slung over his shoulder and a couple of bottles in his hand. He seems unsure of himself as he raises the bottles in greeting. "Hey, hope ya don't mind me crashing yer party."

Violet and Alex exchange a look before she tosses her napkin on the table and pushes her chair back. "Of course not! We're glad you decided to come."

Lance sets the bottles on the table, and I notice his raw knuckles.

Violet takes his battered hand in hers and inspects it briefly. "Why don't we drop your stuff inside?"

"Sure."

She puts her hand on his elbow and leads him toward the cottage, glancing over her shoulder once at Alex before they disappear inside.

"It has to be Tash. She must've called," Randy mutters.

"I think she was in town," Alex says quietly.

"Shit." Miller picks up the closest bottle. It's expensive scotch. "We're gonna have to make sure he doesn't chug this whole thing."

"It's all right. Vi's pretty good at talking him down," Alex says.

A few seconds later, a door on the other side of the cottage opens and closes, and we hear Lance and Violet walking down to the dock. I glance over at Alex. Despite his jealous streak, he doesn't look worried; he just seems sad. It makes me wonder what Lance hides under that front of his.

MISSING

RANDY

O nce dinner is cleaned up, Sunny brings out the baby and bridal magazines. I'm not big on either since I don't have a vagina, so I make my way down to the water to check on Lance. Based on the state of his knuckles, he's had one of his meltdowns. Solar lights mark the path, and soft recessed lights line the edges of the dock. I want to say I trust Lance with Violet, especially since Alex does, but I'm not sure if I do. So I'm bringing them drinks. I know Lance officiated their wedding, but it's hard to forget all the parties and bunnies from last season. He's done some things that are on the edge. He's my friend, but he's not in a good headspace, judging by the state of his hands.

He and Violet are sitting cross-legged, facing each other.

Lance's head is bowed, and his hands are in his lap. He looks like a massive kid.

They look my way when my flip-flops slap on the wood. "We're starting the campfire soon." I offer them each a beer.

Violet shakes her head as she unfurls from her seated position. Standing, she extends a hand to Lance. "You coming?"

"In a bit."

She touches his shoulder. He tenses at the contact, but remains still.

"Thanks." His head stays bowed.

"You don't have to thank me. You know we're here for you." As she passes me she whispers, "You should stay with him."

I drop down beside him and hand him a beer.

He takes it and clinks it against mine. "You checking up on me?"

"Yup."

"I know I'm an asshole, but I would never make a move on Violet. Or any of my friends' women."

I feel bad that he believes this to be the first assumption I came to, and that he's correct. "You're not an asshole, Lance."

"Yeah, sometimes I am." He looks up at the stars and then at me. "But I mean it; you don't have to worry about your girl with me. I won't ever touch a woman who owns someone else's heart —not on purpose anyway. That's cruel."

He looks away and rolls his bottle between his hands. We're silent for a minute while I process what he's said. I wish I was better with words.

"I don't think it would ever be intentional. Sometimes lines get blurred without us even realizing it." I know all about that. Lily and I started out as a casual hook-up, but that changed pretty damn fast, and I almost fucked it up more than once. Lance was part of the reason I didn't, and lucky for me, Lily's a patient, understanding woman. Patience and understanding don't apply in this situation, though.

"I dunno." Lance drops his head. "But Alex and Violet are

solid. That's the only reason I can talk to her. That woman is devoted. What she went through with him earlier this year? She proved herself. She might say ridiculous shit a lot, but she's made for this life. She's got balls. Besides, Alex threatened to murder me a long time ago if I so much as lay a finger on her. We've got a good understanding." He downs half of his beer.

"You don't ever worry that you're gonna start having feelings for her that you shouldn't?"

Lance laughs.

I back track. "I'm not saying you shouldn't talk to her; I just don't want things to get complicated for you."

"Violet would see that coming before it happened. She's like family. Like a sister, you know? Besides, I'm not really interested in the good girls."

I nod to his now-bandaged hands. "You see Tash? Is that what happened here?"

"Yeah. You'd think I'd learn, but I don't." He drains the rest of his beer in one gulp.

"You need to quit her like a bad habit," I say. "She kind of *is* a bad habit, eh?"

"I know." His nod is solemn, but the way his shoulders hunch forward tells me more about how he's doing than his words.

This girl has wrecked him, more than once. I don't get why he keeps letting her do it. "What happened between you two?"

"Too much and not enough." He holds up his empty bottle. "I need another beer."

That's as far as our conversation is going to go. I follow him back to the cottage, and we all get shitfaced at the fire—except Sunny and Miller. He stays sober out of solidarity until she's ready for bed, which is much earlier than the rest of us.

Less than an hour after they disappear upstairs, Miller comes back out and ties one on. It's good for Lance, since that means he's not feeling like a seventh wheel with no one to go to bed with later.

70

The girls are sitting on chairs, taking a million selfies, while Miller roasts his fifth hot dog. Sunny being in bed means it's a Miller meat free-for-all.

"Oh, no, my battery died." Lily gives me her drunk pouty face. "Can I borrow your phone?"

It's cute, but I'm hoping she's drunk enough to want to get her uninhibited freak on, yet not so drunk that she passes out before we even get our clothes off.

"Yeah, of course, luscious." I pat my pockets, then remember I didn't have it with me this afternoon. "It's probably in the truck. I can go have a look for it, if you want."

"Don't worry about it. I'll send you my pictures." Violet has a serious slur.

I cut Lily off around one o'clock, because she's getting bleary eyed, and hangovers hit her hard. We don't go to bed until after three in the morning, and when we do, we leave Lance and Miller out there alone. I make sure Lily takes aspirin and drinks a boatload of water before we get into bed. We have slightly uncoordinated, lazy sex and then pass out hard.

No one gets out of bed before ten the next morning, except Sunny. I'm up before Lily, and I don't bother her with my hard-on. Instead I take care of my own business in the bathroom. Usually I pick one of our recent videos and play it on repeat while I jerk off, but today I'm forced to use my imagination. It works, but it takes longer. I need to check the truck for my damn phone. Also, my hands aren't as soft as Lily's, so that makes it less pleasant than, say, her hands, or her mouth, or her sweet, sweet pussy.

When I venture out, Sunny's in the kitchen cutting fruit. Actually, *cutting* is the wrong word. She's hacking at it like she's trying to machete her way through a forest, not slice a melon. Violet's sitting at the island, her head resting on the counter, a glass of juice in one hand.

"Morning," I say.

Sunny raises her knife in greeting but doesn't turn around.

71

I take a seat beside Violet. "Feeling rough?"

"Shhhh. Too loud, Horny Nut Sac."

"That bad, eh?"

"I killed half my brain cells last night."

"I guess it's a good thing you're smart, and you can afford to lose a few."

"Not smart enough to avoid shooters, apparently. They're a lot like anal: it seems like a good idea at the time, but the actual execution and the aftermath aren't really all that awesome."

"Uhh…" I'm not sure I want to know more about that statement, including whether it's from actual experience or just Violet being Violet.

"Not that I've had anal. I mean, obviously Alex wants to go where no man has gone before with more than a finger, but I'm still on the fence." She moves her head a little and tries to get the straw in her mouth.

"I'm pretty sure that overshare was meant for Miller, not me."

"Meh. You're almost like an extension of each other for me now." She takes a small sip of her juice. "Can I ask you something?"

"Sure. But I reserve the right not to answer."

"You ever try to get into Lily's fire exit?"

"What?"

"Her access-denied hole. You ever try to pirate her door number two?"

"You're asking if Lily and I have anal? Don't you think it's a little early in the morning to talk about this?"

"It's never too early to talk about an Area 51 breach. Besides, I'm doing research. Based on the domes you two were using when you first started dating, I think you and Alex have comparable junk."

"Yeah, I'm not answering that question."

"That's fine. I'll ask Lily later."

"Ask me what later?" Lily's hair is still bed-messed. She's

wearing a pair of shorts and a tank. Based on the way her nipples are poking at the thin fabric, she's not wearing a bra.

"Area 51 access," Violet says. "Does Balls have it?"

"I'm not talking about that." She raises her arms over her head and stretches up on her toes, exposing a sliver of stomach I want to lick. "Thanks for making sure I was watered before I fell asleep last night."

"I wouldn't want you to feel like this one." I thumb over my shoulder at Violet, whose eyes are closed again.

She grunts. "Alex fed me aspirin before bed, but I don't think I drank enough water."

I pull Lily between my legs and skim her sides, accidentally brushing a nipple on my way up. She grabs my hand, but I'm fast, so I snag her wrist and drape her arm over my shoulder, pulling her in closer. At the tip of my chin she puts her ear to my mouth. "I can see your nipples through your shirt."

"I can see yours, too," she whispers back.

I glance down to check if that's true. She pulls the arm of my tank to the side so one peeks out.

"Mine aren't nearly as exciting as yours."

"Can you two foreplay somewhere else? I'm trying to be hungover in peace," Violet mutters.

Lily backs up a step. "Need any help over there, Sunny?"

"Nope."

Lily gives me a questioning look, and I shrug, because I seriously have no idea. Sunny's not usually one to be bitchy. That doesn't seem to be the case this morning.

"Maybe Miller's in the doghouse?" I whisper.

If he came to bed drunk, that could explain her less-than-sunny disposition.

Sunny crosses to the fridge and yanks on the door. She roughly opens a crisper, and the contents spill out all over the floor.

Violet groans and covers her ears. I jump up to catch the runaway lemons and a bag of grapes. Sunny bursts into tears.

Lily rushes over to put an arm around her. "Are you okay?"

"I think I'm going crazy!" she sobs.

Lily rubs circles on her back. "It's just the hormones; you're fine."

"I don't know what's wrong with me. Last night Miller came to bed smelling like campfire and hot dogs. I haven't eaten a hot dog since we went on that tour of the meat-packing factory when we were in grade three, remember that?"

Lily nods. "Of course I remember."

"And they showed us how hot dogs are made? They tried to make me eat one, and I threw up all over the table."

"It set off a chain reaction, and six other kids threw up too."

"It was horrible. I was so traumatized. I had no idea what was in a hot dog."

"I know you didn't," Lily says soothingly.

If Sunny wasn't crying, I would be killing myself over this.

"Well, last night I *liked* the smell of hot dogs on Miller even though I know what they're made of. It's not even real meat! It's leftovers. Every time Miller barbecues, I want to get him naked and lick the flavor off his body. I kissed him after he ate that steak last night without even making him brush his teeth first. What's happening to me?"

"It's probably your body telling you you need more iron," Lily says.

I stay crouched on the floor, picking up scattered grapes and trying not to laugh.

"I wouldn't even let him brush his teeth before he came to bed last night, and then he fell asleep on me before we could have sex!" This incites a fresh round of tears.

"I fell asleep on Alex while he was licking my beaver last night. He's pretty mad at me for that," Violet offers.

Okay. "I'm just gonna go—" I set the crisper on the counter with the beat-up fruit. This isn't a conversation I need to be part of. Or want to be, for that matter.

I round the corner and find Lance outside, sitting on one of the Adirondack chairs. "I'm surprised you're awake."

"I've been up for a while. I was gonna go in and make coffee, but then I heard girl-crying and figured it was safer out here. Everything okay?"

"Yeah. No. But it's hormones or whatever. Sunny's having meat guilt."

He clasps his hands behind his head. "Do I even want to know?"

"Probably not."

"We'll just let it go then. You think it'll be clear to go in soon? I could really use coffee."

"I'd give it another ten minutes. I don't know how long pregnant crying fits last."

Lance shakes his head. "I can't imagine dealing with that. Miller's gotta be some kind of saint to handle all the tears."

I lean against the deck railing and consider that. "He's a patient guy, and Sunny's usually even, you know? People will put up with a lot from someone they care about, especially since this seems to be outside of her control."

"Yeah, I can see that. I guess I've never had anyone give enough of a shit about me to want to put up with my crap for more than a few weeks."

"That thing with Tash went on for a lot longer than that."

"It was just about the fucking, though—and the mind fuck for her—so it doesn't really count."

His phone beeps. He checks the screen and sighs. "Speaking of."

"You should turn that shit off while you're here. Put it out of your head for a couple of days." Kind of like I'm avoiding any additional calls from my dad since my phone is still in the truck.

"That's the problem. She's burrowed her way right in there like a fucking termite, and I can't get her out."

He flips the phone over so it's face down and he can't see the screen. It buzzes again with another message, but he ignores it.

"Hey, you find your phone last night?" he asks.

"No. Shit. I should have a look in the truck. There's some stuff on there I don't want anyone else to see."

"What kinda stuff?"

"Just personal shit."

He pushes out of the chair. "I'll give you a hand."

I can't believe he's not feeling like a bag of shit considering how much he drank last night and how little he's slept.

We walk around to the truck and open the doors. I check all the compartments while Lance looks under the seats.

He holds up a box of condoms. "You still using these?"

"Nah. Lily's been on the pill forever. She's really good about taking it on the regular."

"Wasn't Sunny on the pill when she got pregnant?"

"Yeah, but she had some kind of sinus infection and was taking prescription meds. Apparently they interfere with the pill, and they should've been bagging it."

Lance whistles. "Fuuuuck. I didn't know that."

"Lesson learned, I guess?"

"That's a big-ass, permanent, motherfucker of a lesson."

"Yeah." I nod. "But Miller's rolling with it, and so is Sunny."

"You don't worry Lily's gonna want the same thing?"

"Not right now. Her mom got knocked up at eighteen. I don't think Lily's interested in repeating the cycle."

"Fair enough. Sorry. I didn't mean to get personal on you."

"It's fine. It's not like I haven't thought about it."

Lance tosses the condoms into the glove box. "Just in case you decide you need them."

"Good call."

We switch sides and go through the entire truck one more time, but come up empty-handed. I'm starting to panic a little. My phone has all my contact info in it, not to mention some other things.

"Maybe it's in your room?"

"Yeah. Maybe. It's worth another look." Lance closes up the truck, and I sneak back inside to give our room another pass.

The girls aren't in the kitchen anymore, but I don't stop to find out where they went. I take the stairs two at a time. I check in all the obvious places first: under the bed, in the bed, in the dresser drawers. When I still don't find it, I dump my bag out, rummage through the contents, and check all the pockets, but still nothing. Maybe it ended up in Lily's bag.

I dump hers out on the bed and sift through the frilly, lacy lingerie she has yet to model for me, or let me take off with my teeth, but still no phone.

There are a few extra pockets in her bag, so I unzip those, turn it upside down, and shake it. A bunch of things fall out on the bed. Included is the little vibrating bullet I found in her nightstand drawer a few months back. It comes in handy when I want to torture her with orgasms. Three small bottles of lube—one water-based, one flavored, and a new black one—also litter the comforter. I love how prepared she is, like a regular sex girl scout.

But the item that makes me immediately hard is also brand new and still in the package. Lily bought a butt plug. A fucking hot pink butt plug with a crystal at the end. I try really hard not to imagine what she's going to look like, sound like, feel like when I'm using it on her, but it's impossible. Not once have I ever mentioned wanting to go there with her—though of course I do. I'm a guy. With a dick. I want to put it wherever she'll let me. My motto with Lily has always been: unless she brings it up, I don't.

If she has this, I have to assume, logically, she wants me to use it on her. My hard-on throbs as I consider how amazing that's going to be—and then there's the video I'll make with my phone.

Which I still can't find.

Fuck.

I will my hard-on to go away. It doesn't want to. Now it

wants to get inside Lily. Now it wants me to do dirty, nasty things to my gorgeous girlfriend's ass.

But first I need to find my goddamn phone.

I jam Lily's clothes back in her bag. All the little toys go back in the pockets, except the plug. That I set on top of her clothes and zip up the bag. I want her to know I know she has it. Then I once again will my hard-on to fuck off until I can sort out the missing-phone issue.

"Hey, I've been looking for you!" Lily wraps an arm around me from behind. "Wow. What's going on here?" She gestures to my clothes strewn all over the unmade bed.

"I was looking for my phone."

"Oh. Any luck?"

"Nope."

"Have you checked the truck yet? I thought you left it in there. I forgot my phone charger at home. We can get yours and have a look while we're out there."

I turn and tuck her hair behind her ear. I don't tell her I've already been through the truck twice. I want to have one more look before I let the real worry take hold. "Sure. Let's go."

She threads her fingers through mine. "After brunch we should come up here and have a nap."

"By nap do you mean we should get naked and give each other orgasms?"

Her smile is devious. "You're such a mind reader! That's exactly what I meant."

"I love your version of naps." I kiss her shoulder and tug on her hand. I have a feeling if I don't find this damn phone, the orgasms will not be happening. "Sunny's okay?"

"Yeah. She's fine. Well, as fine as she's going to be until she has that baby. Let this serve as a reminder: never let me forget to take my pill."

"You took it yesterday, right?"

"Oh, yeah. I have three alarms, and I carry a spare pack with me at all times. I take no chances."

I pat her ass and follow her down the stairs. "That's my responsible girl."

Lance and Alex are playing Frisbee with Charlene and Darren in the side yard. Andy chases after the disc with Wiener running between his feet. The little dog snatches the Frisbee when Andy manages to catch it. Violet's lounging in a chair with huge sunglasses and a sombrero pulled low, and Miller is rubbing suntan lotion into Sunny's shoulders. Titan is curled up at her feet.

"Any luck, bro?" Lance calls out.

I shake my head. "Gonna check the truck again."

"Again?" Lily asks. "I thought you hadn't checked yet."

"It doesn't hurt to have another look. I wasn't all that thorough. Don't worry. I'm sure it's in there. I mean, where else could it be?"

"Right? It's not like you could've lost it." I hear a hint of nervousness in her voice. "When was the last time you had it? You took pictures at the convenience store. Did you use it after that?"

"I don't know. Maybe?"

"We should try calling it," Lily suggests after we've been through the entire truck, top to bottom, three more times.

"That's a good idea."

Lance has his phone handy, so he gives mine a call. It goes to voicemail right away, which means the battery is dead.

"Should we call and report it as lost?" Lily chews on her thumb. "I mean, you have a lot of personal information on there. Maybe some things we wouldn't want anyone else to see?"

"Wait a second, don't you two make sex videos on your phones?" Violet asks.

I liked it better when she was nursing a hangover and being quiet.

"They're not sex videos," I counter.

"Really? The one I saw sure looked like a sex video to me," she says.

Lily turns to Violet, incredulous. "Seriously? What the hell happened to the vault?"

Now it's my turn to be pissed. "You showed Violet our private videos?"

"Only the first one you ever made. You remember the one when you woke me up because I fell asleep on you? I thought it was sweet."

"Oh, I remember." For a moment I'm caught up in the memory of that sex-filled night.

"Hold the fucking phone, you two make amateur porn?" Lance looks caught somewhere between a boner and a laugh.

He'd better choose neither.

"It's not porn," I snap.

"You have sex and film it, though?" he asks.

"Just on my phone. Or Lily's sometimes. They're little clips. It's not like they're hour-long marathons or anything," I explain.

"Wow. I mean, shit." Lance blows out a breath and nods his approval to Lily. "You got balls, girl. And I don't mean this guy." He points at me, and then motions to his junk. "But, like, lady balls."

"Will you shut the fuck up right now?" He sure as hell isn't helping the situation.

"Yeah." He shoves his hands in his pockets and rocks back on his heels. "I can do that."

"Okay. Let's not panic, yet." Lily holds up her hands like she's silencing people, except no one is talking. She looks at me. "You erased all the videos on your phone, right?"

"Uhhhh…" I think for a few seconds about what pictures and videos might still be on there. My hesitation must be too long.

"You erased all the videos, right, Randy?" she asks again, more forcefully.

"Well, uh, I…" I stroke my beard. "I didn't erase the one from the changing room yesterday."

Her eyes are wide and doe-like. "Is my face in that one?"

"I don't think so." There are too many people looking at me

to be able to remember the details. My plan had been to get her off and then use the video to help my own situation. Also, Lily in her skating outfit with my fingers all up in her is fucking gold. But not if someone other than me is watching it.

She's gone from calm to high-pitched. "You don't *think* so?"

"I'm not sure."

"Oh my God. Are there any other pictures I should worry about on there? Or videos?"

Lily is approaching an official freak-out. Both Miller and Alex look like they might want to beat me with their hockey sticks.

I tap the bridge of my nose. I don't know whether or not I should be honest, because I'm almost positive there are a few pictures of her without clothes on from last week. Or maybe just a thong. "Maybe one or two?"

"Am I naked?"

"You might be."

"Oh my God. Oh, God. People might see me naked!"

"If it's any consolation, you look great naked," Lance says.

"Seriously, man, I'm about half a second away from punching you in the face." My fists really want to act on their own.

"Wait, when did you see Lily naked?" Miller asks.

Lily strokes her throat absently. "Randy came home from a series of away games. I didn't get the message that Lance was with him until I opened the door."

"You opened the door naked?" Sunny asks. "How come I didn't know about this?"

"Well, technically I wasn't naked. I was wearing a bow. Not that it matters. What matters is that someone might have your phone, and there are pictures of me on it. Naked."

"Lance has a point, though. You look great naked," Violet adds, as if this is going to help.

"When the fuck have *you* seen Lily naked?" I look from Lily to Violet and back again.

Violet gives me the stink eye. "Are you serious with this? You guys probably stand around the locker room comparing your junk and smacking each other on the ass because you scored a goal. We're girls. We get changed in front of each other. They've all seen me trussed up in slutty fetish gear, thanks to this one." She points at Charlene. "Lily had to hold my boobs for me."

"What slutty fetish gear?" Alex asks.

Violet waves him off. "Never mind. We'll talk about that later."

Now I'm curious how many cinderblocks and how much rope I need. "Show of hands. Who *hasn't* seen Lily naked?"

Lily plants her fists on her hips. "Honestly, Randy?"

Only Miller and Darren raise their hands.

I look at Alex. He's bigger than me. I still might have to take him down, though. Or at least try.

He half raises his hand, then brings up the other one as well, as if to ward me off. "She was six. We were kids. It doesn't really count."

"Motherfucker."

"It doesn't matter which of our friends have seen me naked, because if someone has your phone and they jailbreak it, everyone on the goddamn planet is going to see me naked, or partly naked, and being finger-banged by you!"

I don't think she meant to say that last part out loud. She covers her mouth with her palm.

"Nice," Charlene says. Then she turns and whispers something to Darren.

"No one is gonna see that video," I reassure Lily.

"How do you know? You can't even find your damn phone. I teach kids! I can't have internet porn out in cyberspace!"

This is the point where Lily goes into a full meltdown. I've seen her cry a few times, and man, did it ever freak me out, but this is way beyond tears. This is full-on panic-sobbing. I try to hug her, but she pushes me away and goes to Sunny, which makes me feel a million times worse.

"Wait a second. Don't you have a phone locator?" Charlene asks.

"What?"

"That app where you can locate your phone remotely?" Her tone implies I'm stupid for not knowing what she's talking about, but there's been panic, so my head isn't totally clear.

"Fuck! Yes! I do. Someone give me a phone!" I hold out a hand.

Lance hands me his. It takes me two tries to log into my account, but I finally get in there. I'm praying to the internet porn gods that it's not in another state. It shows up as being less than fifty feet away. "It's here!"

"What?" Lily hiccups and seizes the phone so she can have a look.

"It's here. It's on the property." I follow the tracker until I'm in front of Alex's SUV. It takes another five minutes, but I find it stuck between the back seats. The battery is totally dead, but I have it.

Lily's still a blubbering mess, but at least now she's crying because she's relieved, not because she thinks she's started her career as an internet porn star. And I have to say, I'm pretty damn relieved that the relatively small pool of people who have seen her without clothes on is going to remain that way.

As a precaution, we decide it's still a good idea to get a digital camera, as well as a mini video camera, so we can leave the phones out of it. As soon as my phone has enough power to turn on, Lily forces me to delete all of my videos. I don't even get to watch them again, which makes me sad.

But I'm hoping she'll let me make new ones with the video camera we're going to buy.

As soon as we've had breakfast—or more like brunch—I take her into town. While we're shopping, and I'm apologizing and constantly checking for my phone, Lily runs across a vintage-looking Polaroid camera.

"This is awesome!" she says, finally sounding like herself again.

"We should get it."

"That's not necessary. The digital one will be perfect."

Her eyes are still slightly red and puffy, and her lips are swollen—something that apparently happens when she cries. I feel guilty that I caused her worry, and one way to alleviate that is to get her something that will make her happy. If a Polaroid camera puts a smile on her face and keeps it there, I'm getting it.

Lily tries to make me put it back, because it's a little pricey. I cup her chin in my palm and tilt her head up to look in her eyes. I don't care if it makes the store clerk uncomfortable.

"I want all the good memories from this weekend captured, and I like that I'll get instant proof of their existence every time you take a picture with this."

She lets me take the camera from her and give it to the guy behind the counter, who sets it next to the video camera and digital camera we selected. Then I kiss her, softly and without tongue, before I turn back to the guy, who now looks like he's about to have a heart attack. Possibly from our PDA. Whatever.

I buy twenty packs of Polaroid film because we still have the rest of today and all day tomorrow to make a bunch of awesome memories. Also, I have plans for the bedroom tonight.

7

AREA 51
DISCOVERIES

LILY

O n the way back to Alex's cottage, Randy finds an off-roading path. He parks the truck and apologizes for scaring the crap out of me with the phone fiasco by using his tongue and his amazing cock. I'm grateful for the apology *and* the phone not being lost.

Beyond the humiliation of having our very prolific sex life broadcasted all over the internet, I can't even imagine the backlash from the bunnydom. Since I started dating Randy, the bunnies have been guzzling Haterade something fierce. It got worse when he moved me into his house.

I used to think it was crazy how magazines would feature pictures of celebrities grocery shopping, or walking up the steps to their front porch. Like, seriously, who cares what grocery store people shop at? Now that I'm the one people are hypothesizing about, I can tell you a lot of people do care.

I realized this when all of a sudden Randy and I were the focal point of hockey-fanatic speculation: I was pregnant. I'd blackmailed him into letting me move in. We'd secretly gotten married—that came on the heels of Alex and Violet's impromptu Vegas wedding, so it was the least farfetched of all the possibilities. My personal favorite was that we were somehow related and having an incestuous, torrid affair. Most of it I let roll off my back. But sometimes it was hard to take. Sometimes it still is.

So while I'm learning how to handle social media with some level of grace, there's no way in hell I'd ever want those little videos Randy and I make—for and with each other—to go anywhere beyond us. The exception being the first one he ever sent me, which I shared only with a couple of friends. That was the night I started to fall in love with Randy, and he with me. I see it every time I watch that clip. It's in his eyes, in the soft way he looks at me and touches me.

Everyone's down at the dock when we get back to the cottage. Randy's already in his swim shorts, so he sends me up to the room to get changed on my own. That's okay since I had a shot of moody dick on the way home.

I come down in a string bikini chosen with the help of Violet and Charlene on a recent shopping trip. It's not my usual style. There isn't much in the way of fabric, and half my bum is on display, but they both agreed it's sexy, so I bought it. I pull a cover-up over it so I don't feel quite so self-conscious, throw a couple extra towels in my beach bag, and join the rest of our friends.

Randy's already getting acquainted with the Polaroid camera. I sneak up behind him as he snaps a selfie and snatch the picture from the camera.

"Hey! Gimme that!" He grabs for me, but I jump out of reach. He can't really come after me since he's surrounded by developing photos on his armrests and Wiener is in his lap.

"I'll give it to you in a minute."

He snaps a picture of me. "What's under that cover-up?"

"What do you think?" I wave the picture around in the air like I've seen people do.

"That doesn't actually make them develop any faster," Lance says.

"It doesn't?"

"No, but if it makes you feel good to dance around like that, far be it from me to tell you to stop."

He grins, and Randy takes a picture. I wish he could capture Lance's accent in that image, or the teasing in his voice. He's a lot more relaxed today than he was when he arrived last night.

Hangover recovery is in full effect. Miller's asleep in a lounge chair with a hat over his face. Sunny's seated beside him with a bottle of sunblock that she sprays over him to prevent his fair skin from burning. When she sees me, she poses beside him, raising his hand in a mock wave so Randy can get another shot.

"Oh, get one of me and Sunny! We're bathing suit boob twins today!" Violet runs over and pulls her cover-up over her head, then helps Sunny do the same.

Randy hands me the camera. "I like my teeth where they are, especially since only a couple of them aren't mine."

"Good call, Ballistic. You're learning," Alex calls from the boat. He's setting up the water ski rope.

Sunny and Violet are wearing the same bathing suit, except Sunny has on the white version and Violet is wearing red. The Chicago logo is emblazoned as a pattern on the top, and a large logo decorates the front of the crotch. Violet turns around so I can get a picture of her backside, which reads "Mrs. Waters." Sunny adjusts the right butt cheek, but it still isn't doing the best job of covering Violet's ample assets. All the guys except Alex are busy looking anywhere but at Violet's bum.

I pass the camera back to Randy and check out his selfie now that it's had a chance to develop. It's probably one of the best pictures he's ever taken. He's wearing his signature smirk and looking directly at the camera like he's about to get up to no good—in my pants. Or my bikini bottoms, as it were.

"Let's see that one." He pulls on my cover-up, trying to get me to come closer.

"You can't have this back." I hold it face down to my chest.

"It's that bad?"

"No. I love it that much."

"Well, now I need to have a look." He reaches for it and slides his other hand under my cover-up to grab a handful of bum. His brow furrows, and he lifts the hem, peeking underneath. "Whoa. Where's the rest of this?" He skims the edge of the bottoms with a fingertip.

"There is no rest of it."

"Maybe you should put on the one from yesterday again."

"I can't. It's dirty." Damn it. I knew this bathing suit was too much—or too little, actually. I shouldn't have caved when Violet and Charlene told me to buy it.

"I'll be making sure this one's too dirty to wear again, too," he says.

"Who wants to go water skiing?" Alex yells.

I raise both hands in the air and wave them around. "Me!"

Randy puts his hands on my ass, like he's pretending *he's* my new bathing suit. I smack his hands away and tuck the picture he's forgotten about into my bag, carefully storing it between the pages of a book. I'm worried about Randy's reaction when he sees the entirety of this bathing suit. Taking a deep breath, I pull my cover-up over my head and toss it at him. His mouth drops open, and he makes these weird flailing hand gestures. They scare Wiener, who jumps to the dock and starts barking.

"I can't—you gotta—" He shakes his head, balling my cover-up in his lap.

"Want to spot me?" I ask.

"I'm gonna need a minute."

Lance and Darren laugh.

Randy runs a rough hand through his hair. "I feel like it's freshman year of high school all over again."

"What?" I cover my boobs. They haven't grown since grade nine.

"He's got a chubby. Like when one of the cute girls got up and sharpened her pencil and the guys couldn't get out of their desks for ten minutes afterward," Lance says.

"And then it was a competition to see who could get the bathroom pass," Darren adds.

"I can totally see Romance whacking off in the boys bathroom, but I feel like you might've enjoyed spending the day with blue balls," Violet says.

"No one enjoys spending the day with blue balls. Not even me," Darren replies.

I take the skis and a lifejacket from Alex and suit up.

"You wanna drop one?" he asks.

"Let's see how I manage on two first."

Randy seems to feel ready now—he's traded my cover-up for a towel in front of his junk—and he and Violet decide to be my spotters. Randy pretends like he brought the towel in case I can't handle it out there, but that's ridiculous because I'm more than capable of water skiing.

It doesn't take me long to get the hang of it again. After a quick tour, I decide to drop a ski. I'm feeling rather confident, and part of me wants to show off in front of Randy.

Everything is fine at first. I drop the ski no problem, but we run right into a huge wake from a boat coming from the other direction. Alex tries to minimize the waves, but I'm unprepared. The tip of my ski dips under the wake instead of cutting through it, and my foot pops free of the binding. I let go of the rope before I'm dragged down. Instead, I do a few cartwheels across the surface before I somersault twice and go under. As soon as I break the surface, I raise my arm to signal I'm okay.

Randy's standing up, hand in his hair. It drops when he sees me waving. My ski is a long way away, so I stay put while Alex drives over to get it and then swings around to me.

"Nice wipeout! That was impressive. I bet you have the cleanest vagina ever now!" Violet says.

"At least I didn't give myself an enema."

"You wanna get in the boat or try getting up on one ski?" Alex asks.

I can tell Randy would like me to get back in the boat, so I'm about to do the opposite when I realize it's feeling a whole lot free on my bottom half. "Uhh..." I swim in a circle, looking for a scrap of pale pink fabric, but all I see is navy water. "I may have lost my bottoms."

Alex purses his lips, maybe because he's embarrassed, maybe because he's trying not to laugh at my expense. "In the boat it is, I guess."

"Well, that gives new meaning to being blown out of the water," Violet snickers.

"It's a good thing I brought a towel, huh?" Randy holds it out to me as I climb the ladder.

I grab it and wrap it around my waist. "You think you're so funny."

"At least now I don't have to fuck you in a mud puddle to make that bikini unwearable."

After I change my bathing suit, we spend the next couple of hours taking turns water skiing. Violet gives up after three tries and goes tubing instead.

When we run out of gas, the guys go back to playing Frisbee with the dogs, while me and the girls go for another round of flipping through baby and wedding magazines. It's an amazing day. I feel incredibly blessed to have such wonderful friends. I'm even grateful for Benji, my ridiculous ex. If he hadn't been a total asshole a year ago, Randy might never have walked in on me in the bathroom, weed whacking my forest legs. Then I wouldn't have had the opportunity to fall in love with him.

Randy and I don't get any alone time until late in the afternoon. Everyone's tired from all the sun, so we disappear into our rooms for downtime before we start dinner. I flop face down on the mattress. There's some rustling around from Randy on the other side of the room, but I'm surprisingly exhausted. I close my eyes and debate whether or not I can catch a two-minute nap before we get naked.

Something hard hits me in the shoulder, and something else ricochets off my arm. I remain immobile, my face mashed into the comforter. I don't think I even have the energy to turn my body ninety degrees so my head is on a pillow and my feet aren't hanging off the edge.

The bed dips and Randy's body covers mine. He's naked and hard. I'm not surprised.

He noses my hair out of the way. "You're not thinking about napping, are you?"

"What if I was?" I mumble into the comforter.

"I can think of a few things that would be way more exciting than napping." Randy rolls his hips, his erection nestled between my butt cheeks.

"Like a game of Crazy Eights?"

He nips my shoulder and nudges my cheek with his fore-head, like he's trying to get me to turn my head. I don't move at all, keeping my face hidden in the bedding. It's not easy to breathe, but I really am that tired. It doesn't mean I honestly want to take a nap before we have the sexy times, it just means I'm psyching myself up. The apology sex was an appetizer; Randy's going to want to put on a serious performance. That means a lot of orgasms are coming my way.

"I found some interesting items in your bag when I was looking for my phone earlier," he murmurs.

"If you want me to wear sexy lingerie, you're going to have to put it on me. I don't even think I can move my arms." I have no idea if he can understand a word I'm saying since I'm speaking to the mattress.

"The sexy lingerie is nice, but that's not what I'm talking about."

I mentally review the contents of my bag. I don't remember putting anything exciting in there, apart from my bullet, but that's nothing new. "What kind of interesting items?" I turn my head to the side and blow my hair out of my face.

Randy pushes up on his arms and moves the remaining strands out of the way.

A package comes into my field of vision.

"Oh, shit," I breathe. I'm not even remotely tired anymore.

He rolls his hips against my ass again. "Wanna tell me about this?" His voice vibrates with excitement.

Holy mother, he wants to invade my ass. Not once has he ever tried to go there. I mean, obviously when we have sex doggy style, he'll slide his cock between my bum cheeks before he makes a home out of my vag, but in the year we've been together, he's never tried to get into the Area 51 zone, as Violet calls it.

"Umm…" The last time I used this bag was on our Vegas trip, months ago, when Alex and Violet got married. We went to a sex shop. I'd totally forgotten about the butt plug.

I've had a vibrator for a few years, because I have needs. I have a fairly high sex drive, and my ex-boyfriend did not. I needed to take care of myself on a regular basis. But backdoor anything has never been on my radar—not until I started hanging out with Violet and Charlene.

Randy's nose brushes my cheek. "Lily? Did you buy this because you want me to use it on you?"

"Charlene got that for me."

"Charlene bought you a butt plug?" He doesn't sound particularly impressed.

"Um…we went to a sex shop while we were in Vegas, and Charlene bought one for all of us. Kind of like a party favor." My voice goes up at the end, turning it into a question.

"You've had this since Vegas?" Now he sounds shocked.

"I forgot it was in there."

"So it wasn't meant as a surprise?" That's one-hundred-percent disappointment, right there.

"Not really, no."

"Oh. Okay."

I consider for a moment whether or not this is something I want to try. I mean, obviously not butt sex, but, like, butt stuff. My magic marble is lit up like fireworks, and that's based on Randy's excitement alone.

He scoots over, like maybe he's about to get up. I grip his wrist—the one attached to the tattooed hand holding the still-packaged butt plug.

"But we can try it out," I say.

He doesn't make a move. "It's okay if it's not something you're into."

"Is it something you'd be into?"

This time he rolls to the side. I glance down at his massive hard-on with the glistening tip. I don't think he actually needs to answer my question.

He caresses my lip with his thumb. "Not if you'd only be doing it because you think it's something I want. I just thought you brought it with you for a purpose. But if it wasn't inten-tional, I can forget it even exists."

I snort. "Like hell you can."

"Okay, maybe not, but if you decide you never want it to come out of the package, that's cool."

I trace a line on his tattooed arm. "And if I decide I do?"

"That's cool, too."

"Have you ever..." I drop my gaze from his, focusing on the landscape decorating his arm instead. Randy's had a lot of sex with a lot of different partners. Before me.

"Does it matter?"

"No. I guess not."

Randy scoots closer until his nose touches the end of mine.

Then he backs off and puts his finger under my chin. "Look at me, Lily."

I lift my eyes to meet his.

"How do I feel about you?"

"You love me," I whisper.

His smile is soft, warm. "That's exactly right. I've never felt about anyone the way I feel about you. Do you know what that means?"

"That you love me a lot?"

He chuckles. "It means the sex we have is different, because it's more. You get what I mean?"

I nod.

He presses a gentle kiss to my lips. "So whatever you want from me, I'll give you, but only because it's what you want, not because you think it's what I want. Okay?"

"Okay."

I ease my body against his, bringing our mouths together. I hook my leg over his hip, feeling the hot, hard press of his cock against my stomach. We kiss like that for a few minutes, soft and easy, hot tongues dancing.

"Randy?"

"Yeah, baby." He skims my side with a light finger.

"Let's pretend like I meant to surprise you."

AREA 51
BREACH

RANDY

There are moments in life a person never forgets, good and bad. My first goal, nearly having my dick decapitated, being drafted to the NHL, winning the Stanley Cup, and telling Lily I loved her for the first time all fit into this category.

The first time your girlfriend tells you she wants to let you near her ass also earns a special place in the memory bank of Holy Fuck.

Until I found the plug in her bag, I'd assumed—with the way those girls talk about Area 51 and its access-denied status—that it was forever a no-go. Her reaction when I first showed it to her seemed to confirm this. I'm also aware that I've got more going on in the dick department than the majority of guys, so unless Lily is secretly an anal porn star, I'm not getting access.

Except now I am. Maybe not with my cock, but this is a step in that direction. A small, pink step with a jeweled end. It's gonna look fantastic peeking out of her ass.

I'm so fucking excited, I think my dick is going to explode.

I cup her cheek—the one on her face. "Are you sure?" I have to ask. This isn't like a new sex position. This is way more awesome, and it requires a hell of a lot more trust—or a chick who's been down the anal road a lot. Since the latter isn't a reality, the former is where my concern lies.

"Yes. Totally."

I kiss her again, aware she has to be nervous. I want this to be a good experience for her. I don't have to ask if it's something she's done before; based on her reactions thus far, this is unexplored territory. That I get to do this first with her makes it a really big fucking deal.

"I'm gonna make this so good for you, luscious."

"You always make me feel good." The tremor in her voice gives away both her excitement and her trepidation.

We make out for a while, and I keep one hand on her ass, just kneading. She's rubbing herself on my cock, the satiny fabric of her bikini bottom the only thing in the way. She's trying to get off, but without a seam, I don't think she'll have much success. Which is good. I need her excited and at the edge. She makes a plaintive noise, fingernails digging into my skin.

I break the kiss. "Let's get you naked."

"Best idea ever."

She starts to roll onto her back, but I turn her the other way so she's on her stomach instead. I pull the ties on her top and the strings on the bottoms. Then I start with the teasing. I kiss a path down her spine. When I get to her ass, I start biting, massaging, caressing. I slip my fingers between her legs and circle her clit, then quickly withdraw them.

"Randy," she moans, lifting her ass off the mattress.

"Yeah, baby?"

"I wanna come."

"Is that right?"

She groans and tries to slide her hand under her body so she can give herself what I won't yet.

I straddle her legs in one quick move and grab both of her hands. She moans again and bucks underneath me, like she's trying to get me off of her. Threading my fingers through hers, I stretch out, keeping her legs tight together by planting a knee on either side of her thighs. This time there's no bathing suit to prevent me from sliding my cock along her ass.

Her fingers tighten around mine. "Oh, fuck."

"That's the plan. Eventually." I claim her mouth. Every stroke of my tongue and roll of my hips is meant to remind her what she doesn't have yet, and wants.

I break the kiss and sit back on my knees, easing one between her thighs now. She immediately tries to wiggle her way down the bed so she can rub up on it. I give her ass a light slap, and she gasps, looking over her shoulder.

"Just wait for it, baby. I promise it'll be worth it."

Grabbing a couple of pillows, I slip an arm under her waist and prop her up. Then I get the small bottle of lube designed specifically for this scenario and pour a thin stream along the cleft of her ass. That gets me another groan.

With the tip of the plug, I stroke from her clit to her ass. I'm rewarded with a gasping breath and a shift of her hips. I make slow circles, easing the tip inside, watching carefully for signs of discomfort or uncertainty. There aren't any. When it's evidently not enough, she lifts her hips, so I go a little deeper with the plug. Lily sucks in a sharp breath.

"Too much?" If I was using my finger I'd be about two knuckles deep by now. There's less than an inch to go.

She gives her head a furious shake. "Not too much. God, Randy, I wanna come."

"I know. I want you to come, too." I give her a little more, and she arches her back, pushing it in the rest of the way for me. I knead her ass and stare, because Jesus, this is a million times better than any porn I've ever seen. It's complete vulnerability and trust on her part.

She reaches back and skims the jeweled end with shaking fingers. Looking over her shoulder at me she asks, "Will you take a picture so I can see what it looks like?"

And I almost blow my motherfucking load right there. "Fuck, Lily, of course. Stay just like that." I nab the Polaroid camera, which I had the good sense to leave on the nightstand. I snap a picture and toss the developing image to Lily. Then I grab the digital camera—because fuck just Polaroids for this—and take about twenty pictures. I switch to the video camera and hit record as I rub slow, gentle circles around her clit. And orgasm one hits her.

Lily comes on a seriously loud moan. The picture she's holding crumples in her fist, and she shudders violently. When it seems like it's mostly over, I cover her body with mine again, aware my weight will put pressure on the plug.

She mashes her face into the comforter to muffle a string of profanities. I have a feeling our sex life is about to ramp up a few notches, if this is any indication of how much experimenting Lily's cool with.

I prop myself up on one elbow, kissing along her jawline. "Lift your head for me."

It takes her a few seconds to comply, which is understandable since she's still shaky from the orgasm. I hit record again as I brush stray hairs away from her face. Her eyes are glassy, her cheeks gorgeously flushed, lips parted.

"Did you come, baby?" I ask on a whisper.

She nods.

"Was it good?"

She tries to turn her head to look at me, so I encourage her to look at the camera again.

"You're recording this?" she asks breathlessly.

"I'll delete it when we're done if you want me to."

"Did you get me coming?"

This time I nod and kiss her cheek. "Do you want to see?"

She bites her lip, white teeth sinking into soft pink flesh, and nods. So I show her what it looked like from my perspective. Fifteen seconds in, she stops watching and grips my hair, seeking my mouth. She's aggressive and needy, rubbing her ass on my cock, asking me to fuck her.

"Let me use my fingers first." I shift to the left, kissing her neck while I finger-fuck her. She comes twice, hard and fast, and then she's begging for my cock again. It's so hot to see her like this: absolutely uninhibited, losing control and loving it.

She pushes up on all fours when I get into position behind her. I tap the plug, and she moans. "You want this out before I fuck you?"

"No. Leave it in."

"You sure?" Sweet Christ, let her be sure.

"Positive."

"Just tell me if it's too much or it gets uncomfortable, okay?"

"'Kay."

I run the head of my cock from her clit all the way to the little plug and back again a few times before I head to the Vagina Emporium and give her the tip.

"How's that feel?"

"Full. Good."

"You want me to keep going?"

"Please."

"I'm probably not going to last very long, Lily. The view is fucking spectacular."

"Picture, please," she rasps.

I pick up the Polaroid again and snap one, tossing the undeveloped image to her. "Try not to ruin this one."

She snickers, then sucks in one of those high-pitched breaths when I ease in farther. I must not be giving it to her as fast as she wants, because she rocks back until I'm all the way inside her. Now, Lily's always been a nice, snug fit, but this is way more intense. Based on the way she's breathing, and the nearly constant moans, I'm betting it's the same for her.

"How's that feel now?" I put my thumb on the jeweled base and push a little.

"Unreal."

I go slow at first, giving her time to adjust. When her arms start to give out, I bar one of mine across her chest to keep her from face-planting into the mattress. Also, we have a great view of what's going on in the mirror over the dresser. Lily moves my palm to rest under her chin and bites the end of my finger when I skim her lips.

"My sexy, sweet girl." I kiss below her ear. "You look so good all filled up like this."

I take her mouth, swallowing moans as she comes again, and it doesn't take long before I follow her. Then I roll to the side and wrap my arms around her, tucking her in close.

After a few quiet seconds she says, "I think it's safe to say I'm definitely into ass stuff."

"That's good, 'cause I'm totally into your ass."

She traces the lily tattoo on the back of my hand. "I'm pretty sure that was the best sex ever in the history of fucking."

I smile into her shoulder. "Totally agree."

"Thanks for that."

"For you? Anytime."

We lie there for a while, sweaty and sated, until Lily says, "I need to unplug my ass and have a shower."

"I bet that's a sentence you never thought you'd say."

"Before you? Not in a million years." She moves off the bed. "You coming to help me, or am I on my own?"

"Oh, I'm coming." I fucking love this woman so much.

WE STAY UP TOO late and sleep in the next morning, even though it's our last day. Lily wakes me up with a blow job, and we spend the day down at the dock—not drinking, just relaxing. Lance takes off late in the afternoon. Text messages have kept him distracted most of the day. I assume it's Tash, getting under his skin again, but he's tight-lipped about it, so I can't say for sure.

The rest of us pack up after a dinner of leftovers and don't hit the road until nearly eight. None of us wants to leave any earlier than we have to, but all the girls have to work tomorrow, so it's time to get back to the city. Halfway home, my phone rings.

"Wanna see who that is for me?" I ask Lily.

She checks and makes a face. "It's your dad. Do you want to take it?"

"Nah. Don't bother. Let it go to voicemail."

She doesn't ask questions, just sends the call straight to my messages. Right away he calls a second time, and we ignore it. Lily knows my relationship with my dad is shitty, and she gets it since she doesn't have one at all with her father. Her mom's current boyfriend, Tim, seems to be a decent guy, though, even if he's shirtless half the time we see him.

It's been an awesome weekend. I don't want to ruin the end by fielding another call from my dick of a dad asking for a place to crash.

"He's not in town, is he?" Miller asks from the backseat. Sunny fell asleep on his shoulder a few minutes after we hit the road.

"I don't know. I don't have time to deal with him right now, not with training starting next week," I say.

Miller nods his understanding.

I'm antsy the rest of the way home. I need to listen to that message and make sure my mom knows not to take my dad's calls in case he's decided to come to Chicago despite my not being there. They haven't been together for more than a decade, but he still tries to see her and pull his bullshit when he can. She might not take it from him, but it affects her. She gets stressed, worried that he's going to stop by the house and pull one of his stunts. I think back in the early days, when they'd just split up, he did that to her a lot—making promises, trying to win her back. She doesn't need that kind of head game, especially not after this many years.

I'm seriously hoping he's not in town. I don't want Lily to meet him. Ever.

It's after ten by the time we drop off Sunny and Miller and their dogs at home. Lily's relaxed and quiet beside me; the sun and sex have worn her out. At least she doesn't have to work until eleven tomorrow, so she can sleep in.

Lights illuminate the kitchen when we pull into the driveway. I don't remember leaving them on, but it's entirely possible I did since I was in a bit of rush, wanting to get to the arena before Lily had to be on the ice with that Finlay guy. Who I still don't really like for no reason other than he gets to put his hands on my girl. I get our bags from the back of the truck while Lily gathers up the items scattered around the cab.

She still seems pretty awake and cheery, despite the long day. I'm hoping a shower and some slow, easy sex will round out this kickass weekend. Lily punches in the code, and I open the door. The TV's on in the living room.

"Did you leave the TV on all weekend?" Lily leans against the wall so she can toe her shoes off without dropping her armload of miscellaneous stuff.

"I don't—" A pair of bare feet hang over the edge of my couch. "Fucking shit." I slam the door.

Lily jumps, and the items tumble from her arms to the floor. I drop our bags and immediately shift her behind me. My first instinct is to walk right back out the door and drive her home, except she is home. Because she lives here. With me. And I don't want anything to change that.

The feet disappear, and a head pops up.

"Randy, who—" Lily begins.

"Hey, kiddo, I tried to call you a couple of times, but I guess…" My dad pauses, his bloodshot gaze shifting to Lily. A slow, sloppy grin spreads across his face. "You've been busy. Sorry, buddy. I didn't mean to interrupt you and your chippy."

RANDALL BALLISTIC (SR) IS AN ASSHOLE

LILY

R andy puts a protective arm around me and pulls me into his side, angling us so I'm half hidden from the leering man. I don't need to ask who this is. It's pretty obvious it's Randy's father. Even without the "kiddo" and "buddy" references, one look answers so many questions about Randy's insecurities when it comes to being like his dad.

It's honestly like looking at Randy, except a good twenty years later and without a beard. Randall Ballistic, Sr., could be a handsome, distinguished man—if he gave a shit about himself. It's clear he doesn't.

He's wearing a stained, wrinkled T-shirt and a pair of Randy's pajama pants, which means he went into our bedroom to find them. He's not terribly out of shape, though he stretches the shirt around the middle. His hair is a greasy mess, but it's all there. His appearance isn't the most shocking thing about him.

The bottles lining the table indicate the slur in his speech isn't because he's tired. Oh no, he's drunk—really drunk based on the empties. He seems to have gone through a twelve-pack.

"Lily's my girlfriend, not a fucking chippy," Randy snaps.

This gets me another onceover from Randy's dad. "Whoa, girlfriend?"

Randy's arm tightens around my shoulder. It's like he wants to wrap himself around me, or push me out the door. Of all the parental introductions, this tops the list for the worst.

"How'd you even get in here?"

"Your mom gave me the code. Took a little persuading."

Randy's hold on me tightens further. "You went to Mom's?"

"Nah, I just called." Randall, Sr., uses the arm of the couch to push himself to standing. "Aren't you gonna introduce me to your little girlfriend? Where's your manners, kid?" He stumbles and hits the coffee table with his knee, sending bottles flying. One rolls to the floor and shatters.

"Christ," Randy mutters.

"Ah, it's not a big deal. I'll clean it up." His dad waves him off and tries to step over the broken shards. But he steps right in the middle of the mess instead of around it. He loses his balance and stumbles forward.

"For fuck's sake, Dad." Randy grabs him as he goes down to one knee. Hoisting him up, Randy drags him away from the mess of broken glass and drops him on the floor, propping him against the wall.

"I'll get the first aid kit," I offer.

"It's just a little cut; it's fine," Randall, Sr., says, despite the shard of glass in the bottom of his foot, the gash on his hand, and the steady stream of blood dripping to the floor.

"It's not a little cut; look at how much you're bleeding," Randy snaps.

I leave Randy to deal with his dad while I retrieve the first aid kit. I don't want to be gone long, because I can see how agitated he is over this. I also have a feeling the gash on the bottom of his dad's foot may need stitches.

I return a minute later with dark towels, a washcloth, and the medical kit we keep in the bathroom. Hockey players sustain frequent minor injuries, so we have a vast array of bandages, medication, and ointment.

Randy's dad has one leg crossed over the other. He's trying to dig the shards out with his fingers—there's more than one.

Randy scrubs a hand over his face. "Dad, I need to take you to the hospital; those are too deep."

"It'll be fine once I get the glass out." His fingers are slick with blood, and it's dripping onto the pajama pants he "borrowed" from Randy. I bought them for him for Valentine's Day, along with the cologne and a few other little things. They're probably destined for the garbage now.

"Why don't you let me take a look?" I drop to the floor, holding a folded black towel.

Randy's dad stops digging around. He gives me a sloppy version of a Randy smirk. "Your girlfriend's a nurse?"

"Lily's a figure skater." Randy kneels beside me and takes the kit. "I can do this."

"It's okay, I got it."

"No really, baby, you've got work in the morning. Why don't you get ready for bed or something?"

I can tell it makes Randy nervous to have me anywhere near his dad, but I'm equally nervous about leaving them alone together. Randy looks like he's about to snap.

"I'll clean up some of the mess, okay?"

Randy gives me a vague nod, so I leave them to get the broom from the front hall closet. While Randy picks glass out of his dad's foot, I sweep the floor, then follow with a vacuum and the mop. We won't be walking around barefoot until I go over it again—when it's not approaching midnight. By the time I've finished putting all the empty beer bottles in the recycle bin and tidying the kitchen, Randy's finished gluing his dad's foot back together and picking glass out of his palm, as well.

"I still think you're probably going to need stitches," Randy says.

"It's fine. Just a couple small cuts."

Randy sighs but doesn't argue. Instead he collects the bloody towels and bandages, dumping them in the trash. "I'll set you up in the spare room for tonight."

"I'll make sure the sheets are clean." I already know they are, but Randy's dad's foot is still bleeding, so it's advisable to have dark sheets. I change them from beige to navy.

Randy helps his dad hobble down the hall. I take our bags to the laundry room and leave them there so I can deal with them in the morning. It's midnight now, and while I don't have to work until eleven tomorrow, I don't know what the morning is going to look like with Randy's dad here. The last time he came to see Randy, I remember he stayed for quite a long time. And not because Randy wanted him to.

I'm in the shower when I hear the click of our bedroom door. A few seconds later, there's a knock. "Lily?"

"You can come in!" I peek my head through the gap in the curtains as Randy peeks around the jamb. "You want to join me?"

He nods, locking the door behind him. He strips out of his clothes and climbs into the shower. The first thing he does is wrap his arms around me and press his face against my wet neck.

"I'm sorry," he says.

I run my hands up and down his back. "You have nothing to apologize for."

"Yes, I do. He ruined our fucking weekend with this."

"We had a fantastic weekend. This doesn't change that." I want to reassure him that it's okay, but I understand what he means. All the goodness has been eclipsed by his father's unexpected arrival.

"I changed the damn code so he couldn't get in here. Figures he'd manipulate my mom into giving it to him." He lifts his head. His expression is pained. "I didn't want you to meet him. Not ever. And especially not like this."

"It's okay, baby. You handled it really well."

I know if I'd gotten to choose how Randy and my mom met, it certainly wouldn't have been at my work when my mom surprise-visited me with her new boyfriend—right after I'd spent a night blowing through a box of condoms with Randy. The finale had been sex in the back of Randy's rental Jeep about twenty minutes before my shift started. We made up for a month of not seeing each other in a twenty-four-hour span.

"He's a fucking trainwreck. He comes into my house, eats my food, drinks all my beer, and breaks shit. It happens every damn time." He cups my face in his palms. "In the morning I'm taking him to a hotel. He can't stay here. I don't want you to be alone with him."

"Whatever you think is best." I don't try to dissuade him. That plan sounds good to me, too.

Randy doesn't get agitated like this often, and when he does, he usually has a legitimate reason. Besides, his dad makes me nervous—partly because it's like looking at Randy through an aging mirror. His father's presence also isn't good for Randy's psychological wellbeing, and despite our relaxing weekend (until now) Randy is already on the anxious side.

The shower is functional, not sexual, and Randy puts on boxers before he climbs into bed. He usually goes commando. He wraps himself around me under the covers, but he's not hard, and he doesn't make a move for sex. I wouldn't be worried, as we've had a sex-filled weekend, but I have a feeling the lack of interest is directly related to his dad being here.

There's also no morning sex. Randy's already up and in the kitchen by the time I make an appearance. I remembered to get dressed since we have a houseguest, if you can call his father that. A pot of tea sits on the counter, nestled in its cozy. Randy's sitting at the kitchen table with a coffee and the paper.

He looks up at the sound of my slippers slapping the tile floor. "Hey."

I pad over to him and take a seat in his lap, wrapping my arm around him. "You look tired."

He gives me a small smile. "I didn't sleep very well."

"Maybe you should come back to bed for a while. I don't have to leave for another three hours. We could snuggle."

He drops his forehead into the crook of my neck and rubs his beard along my collarbone. "I like snuggling."

"So do I." I push my fingers through his messy hair. "So that's exactly what we should do."

Before I can further entice him back to bed, and possibly take his mind off the problem still asleep in the spare room, Randy's dad appears in the doorway.

"Oh, hey. Didn't mean to interrupt."

I attempt to get up from Randy's lap, embarrassed for no good reason other than his dad's a parent, but Randy tightens his arm around my waist to keep me there.

Randall, Sr., hobbles over to the coffee. "I didn't think your girlie friend would still be here."

"Lily lives here," Randy says coldly.

His dad stops to look over his shoulder. "Really? That's new."

"Not really. She moved in before the end of the season."

"Oh yeah? Was that around the time your team fucked their chances of getting to the finals?"

Randy huffs. "We had an off season. It happens."

"Maybe you had too many distractions." He pours coffee into a cup and roots around in the cupboard.

I choke back "Fuck you, asshole" and go with, "The sugar's on the counter."

He grumbles something but dumps a couple spoonfuls in his cup and stirs.

"I should get ready for work." I have hours before I need to be ready, but this whole situation makes me uncomfortable. I untangle myself from Randy.

"Oh, so you have a job?" Randy's dad sips his coffee, eyeing me over the rim of his cup. "What's it you do, Lila?"

"Her name is Lily," Randy snaps. "And I told you what she does for a living last night."

"Last night's kinda fuzzy. What kinda job you have?"

"I teach skating lessons."

"Why do you even care?" Randy asks.

"I'm making conversation, getting to know your girlfriend since she lives here and this is the first I've heard of it." Randy's dad's smile is derisive.

"She teaches kids." Randy follows me to the doorway. "Why don't you get ready, and I'll take you out for breakfast and then drop you at the arena. It's just lessons today, right?"

"Mostly. I won't be done until about eight."

I don't want to remind him that I end the day with Finlay again, as there's nothing making Randy happy right now. Giselle won't be back on the ice until later this week. We probably should have talked about that this weekend—Randy's actions in the locker room before and after Finlay's last session, how he managed the introduction—but now is definitely not the time.

"Oh. Okay." The tic in his jaw and flare of his nostrils indicate that this news is not particularly okay, but the conversation will have to wait until we're out of here and away from the current source of angst.

Instead of giving him more words that won't help, I rise up on my toes and draw him down for a soft kiss. He comes willingly, but he's tense and guarded. I leave him with his father.

Running a brush through my hair, I dab concealer under my eyes and toss my makeup bag in with my skating gear. I bring two outfits, because I'll be there most of the day and I don't want to stink by the time it's over. I change my top but keep the leggings, in case Randy decides he wants to take me somewhere semi-nice.

I'm almost ready when Randy's raised voice filters down the hall. "You don't get to come here and say shit like that about the people I love! When I get back, I'm taking you to the hospital to have that looked at, and then I'll drop you off at a hotel."

"You're gonna kick me out? Why, so you don't have to worry about me hearing what's going on with your little chippy when the doors are closed?" His dad's deep, angry laugh slices through the air.

"Call Lily that again and I'm going to give you a real reason to go to the hospital."

"Are you threatening me over a piece of ass?"

"What the fuck is wrong with you?"

There's a heavy thud, and a sound like pictures rattling on the walls follows. I don't know whether to stay where I am or get in the middle of this. I'm not all that interested in managing a brawl in my hallway, but I don't want *two* men who need a trip to the hospital on my hands, either.

"Randy?" I call. I give it two seconds before I open the door and step out into the hall. "Do you know where—" I pause, looking between them.

Randall, Sr., is leaning against the wall, smoothing out his shirt, and my Randy is running a hand through his hair, his jaw tight, the other hand balled into a fist.

"Is everything okay?"

"Yeah." Randy nods, tense. "You need me for something, luscious?"

I scramble for a reason. "Do you know if I left my new leotard in the laundry room? I can't find it in here."

He doesn't hesitate, just nods and holds out his hand. "Let's go look."

I glance at his dad as we pass. His smirk isn't cute like Randy's; it's malicious.

Obviously I don't need another leotard, but there is one

hanging from the drying rack in the laundry room, so I grab it and toss a baseball cap at Randy. "We should go for breakfast now."

"Yeah."

Randy's dad isn't in the hallway or the kitchen, thankfully, as we make our way to the front door. Randy hands me the keys to the truck and tells me to start it, then runs back inside. He's gone too short a time to have committed murder, but that's about the only assurance I have.

I wait until we're away from the house before I ask, "Are you okay?"

"Yeah."

I shift in my seat. "Let me try that again. Randy, are you all right?"

He sighs and taps the steering wheel. If he wasn't driving, his knee would be bouncing like a prostitute on a cock.

"I really thought I'd be able to avoid you ever meeting him."

"I know. It doesn't change how I feel about you now that I have, though."

"He's such a fucking asshole."

"Lots of people are assholes, Randy. It sucks when they're related to us by blood, and we can't pretend we don't know them."

He kisses my knuckles, rubbing them across his cheek. "I love you. So much. I don't want him to jeopardize this."

"He won't. I promise." Words are just words, though. Unless I can reassure him in some other way, his anxiety level is going to remain high, at least until his dad disappears again.

We don't go to a restaurant. Instead we get takeout from our favorite diner and drive to a park near the arena. Randy and I walk to our spot. It's private and secluded. We had sex here once in the middle of the day, hidden in a thicket of trees. Afterward we went home and fucked the night away.

That's not part of the plan today. I don't think sex is even on Randy's mind. That could be a first.

"My dad wasn't always a huge asshole." He takes a bite of his ham and cheese wrap and chews thoughtfully. "When I was little, I remember going to his games. There were a couple of seasons where he got decent ice time. I was maybe five or six. Brynne was, like, tiny, and we'd all go to the home games like the other families. It was good. Things were good."

A butterfly lands on Randy's tattooed hand. "Take a picture," he whispers.

I'm quick to get my phone and snap several before she takes off again, leaving just the two of us.

"We used to shoot the puck around all the time when he wasn't away. He was a great teacher. For a while he was a great dad."

These are the things Randy doesn't talk about much. Most of our conversations about his father have been brief and disparaging.

"When did that change?" I ask.

Randy twirls a lock of my hair between his fingers. "When his career stalled out maybe? No. That's not true. I think when he made it to the top of his game things started to change. The first year he made the NHL, things were good. Great. That was the year we went to a lot of home games." He drops my hair and looks up at the clear blue sky. "But the next year… I started noticing all the women wearing his jersey. The fighting started soon after that. And we stopped going to see him play."

"Do you think that's when your dad started cheating?"

"I don't think I'll ever know for sure when it started. I mean, it could've been going on the entire time. But I assume that's when Mom found out, or put it together or whatever. There were a lot of fights and tears for a few years. I don't think it helped that he stopped getting as much ice time. There was talk about him being traded, or moving back to the farm team. My mom didn't want to move us, and I didn't really get it back then."

"That would've been a lot of turmoil."

"Yeah. It was, even though in the end we didn't have to move.

Then I had that accident, and that was it. My dad moved out. He got traded to another farm team on the West Coast, and we barely ever saw him anymore. It was the hardest on my sister, and, well, obviously my mom. He paid child support and stayed on the farm team for a while, and we all kind of moved on without him. Now he drops back into my life once or twice a year and fucks things up."

"Because he brings back all those memories?"

"And because we're essentially the same person. Sometimes I wonder how my mom can even stand to look at me."

My heart breaks for him. I hate that he carries this burden based solely on what he looks like and his skill set. "You're not the same person, though, Randy."

"In a lot of ways we are."

"I get that it's difficult to separate yourself from him, especially when he shows up and craps all over your life, but you're an incredible man. You're loyal and honest and wonderful. Your personality is nothing like his, and your mom loves you like crazy."

Randy tucks me into his side and rests his chin on top of my head. "I'm worried about the start of the season, Lily. I'm worried about being on the road all the time and you not being with me."

"People choose for themselves whether or not they want to exercise self-control," I remind him.

He presses his lips to my temple. "I don't ever want to hurt you."

I've been waiting for this conversation. It's inevitable. Randy's wanted more and more alone time with me over the past month as off-season wound down and he started gearing up for training. I've realized his anxiety and neediness lately are because of the change that's coming. Soon his schedule will fill up with training sessions and practice. Not long after that, he'll be off on his first series of away games.

I stroke his cheek, amazed that this man can allow himself to be vulnerable with me after everything he's been through. "I don't think you would ever intentionally seek to hurt me, Randy."

"Me neither, but I keep thinking about that time you couldn't make the game last season, and how that bunny wouldn't leave me alone at the bar. I know nothing happened, but if it had, it would've fucked everything up."

"We were still casual then, Randy. Neither one of us had acknowledged how we felt about each other." I know this has weighed on him since the beginning, and his dad being here, along with the changes we're about to face, has stirred it up again.

He sighs. "That's because I was being stupid. I was already all about you, and I still considered it."

"I think you need to let that go. We can't live in a world of what ifs. We weren't ready to face feelings at that point. Denial was safer emotionally for both of us at the time. We're in a different place now; we love each other, and that changes how we manage those kinds of situations."

"My dad loved my mom, and he still managed to fuck that up, though. I don't understand why you'd make that kind of commitment to someone and shit all over it. It's fucked up, isn't it? It's hard to see the way he is now and know at one point he was actually a decent person."

Randy's conflict over this makes me sad for him. It's clear he wants to make sense of it without having all the pieces of the puzzle. He'll only ever had the glossed over and hazy childhood version of events. I guess in a lot of ways not having a father uncomplicates things for me. "I don't know who your dad was when you were younger. I don't know the dynamics of your relationship with him, or how his relationship was with your mom, or what happened exactly to change that, but I do know that you've spent a lot of time afraid of becoming him when really you should focus on being you."

"I just see so much of myself in him; it's hard not to feel like his path is going to be mine."

"You've already made better choices, though, haven't you?"

"Yeah, I guess."

"You need to give yourself more credit, Randy. We've broken the cycles we were following by default before we found each other. Now we've realized there's another way."

He cracks a smile. This time it's real. "Loving you is the best choice I ever made."

"I feel exactly the same way about loving you."

He wraps me up in his warm embrace. I smooth my hands down Randy's back, and it seems at least some of the tension he's been storing there has dissipated. I'm not under some false notion that we've solved this problem with one conversation, but I know talking is progress. As long as we're communicating, I think we can survive his dad's latest ambush—and maybe eventually get to actual healing.

10

GROW
SOME BALLS

RANDY

I drop Lily off at the arena twenty minutes before her first lesson. Instead of going home, I stand at the entrance to the rink and watch her skate for a good half hour. Right now she's teaching three year olds how to stay upright. She's great with kids. Later she'll be dealing with twelve-year-old boys who need to develop ice skills. Their dads always hang out during the lessons. If I didn't have to deal with my own father, so would I.

I'm not happy with the current situation in my house. Our house. Though it's never fun, most of the time I can deal with my dad—his drinking and the asshole comments—but not when they're directed at Lily. I won't risk my relationship with her so he has a place to crash and someone to mooch off. Besides, watching his continued downward spiral is fucking depressing.

I'm already anxious about the start of the season. I don't need his presence making it worse. And that's what he does. He makes things worse. He's all the things I don't ever want to become magnified.

I want to believe what Lily said—that I'm better than he is, and that I'll make better decisions than he did. But it's hard when I think about how he was when I was a kid and what he's become now. I don't understand what caused that change, so I don't know how to guard against it in myself. And while I'm committed to remaining faithful on the road, I have no idea how Lily's going to handle my being away. I've watched more than one of my teammates' relationships implode over the years. I don't want the same thing to happen to us.

I get a message from Lance asking if I want to hit the gym. I fire one back to let him know I'm busy, but I'll catch up with him soon. We have a team meeting in a couple of days since we're gearing up for season training. The long off-season has been good for the team in a lot of ways, even though it sucked to get shut down early in the playoffs. It's also meant more time with Lily and more time hanging out with friends like we did this weekend.

While I'm stoked for the new season, I'm not excited for the travel like I used to be. I now understand my mom's anxiety every time my dad prepared for a series of away games. Her tears when he walked out the door never lasted long; she always pulled herself back together, and we carried on like we always did. But she was different when he was away, and for a long time I didn't get why. Now I do. The why is in my home, probably drinking my booze, even though it's barely noon.

It's in this mood that I arrive back at my house. I don't want to go inside. I don't want to face this issue that looks like me and talks like me. I don't want to deal with the worst-case scenario of my future. But there aren't any other options.

My dad's kicking back on the couch with his wrapped foot

propped on a towel on the armrest. Fresh blood has seeped through the bandage on his heel.

"We gotta go to the hospital. You need stitches."

"It's fine. Get your girlfriend off to work okay?"

"It's not fine. You're bleeding all over the place. Come on; we're going."

He sets his beer next to two empties. "You're in a shit mood."

"I wonder why that would be."

"Look, I had no idea you were playing house with some ch— some girl. It's not like you call me."

"I really don't feel like doing this."

"Doing what?"

"Talking. Let's take a trip to the hospital and get your foot fixed up."

For once he doesn't push it, possibly because I almost punched him out earlier today when he made a dickhead comment about Lily.

We spend nearly three hours in the ER before they even get to us. It would've been a lot longer if I didn't have connections.

Lily messages me while we're waiting—in a different room now, but aside from a quick nurse's assessment, still waiting. She's hoping to get together for a quick dinner before her session with Finlay the fucker tonight. The guy probably isn't that bad, but my stress level doesn't allow for much generosity right now. I'm barely handling the basics. Unfortunately I'm stuck at the hospital at least until they take X-rays of my dad's foot, so I can't go anywhere. I probably won't see her until after he's been humping all over my girl. That makes me pissy. Pissier than I already am.

The X-ray shows that there's still glass in my dad's foot. So they shuttle us back to a room to deal with that before he gets the stitches everyone but him knew he needed. I almost want to tell them not to bother with anesthetic before they go digging around in there. Once he's clear of foreign objects, the doctor stitches him up and gives him a set of crutches. He's supposed to use them for the next few days, otherwise he's liable to break the stitches open. The doctor also wants to see him again in forty-eight hours to check on the healing because the wound was still bleeding pretty good when they were working on him. I assume it has something to do with the blood-thinning properties of all the booze my dad consumes.

The whole thing will probably run several grand since my dad doesn't have health insurance anymore. And he doesn't pretend like he's going to pay me back. Over the past few years, he's probably cost me about thirty grand between the money he borrows and what I dish out for various reasons—hotel bills, hospital visits, other messes to clean up—when he drops by for a visit. I should probably stop helping him out, but if I do, I worry he'll go to my mom, maybe get her to ask me indirectly, since he seems to have no moral compass. The last couple of times he's asked for money he hasn't bothered calling it a loan. I don't question him about his personal financial situation, and I'm certain he knows what mine is; my annual salary is public knowledge.

My dad's looped on painkillers when we leave the hospital, so as much as I want him out of my house, I'd feel like too much of a dick taking him to a hotel for tonight. And yes, it's tonight. The entire afternoon evaporated while we waited in there. Besides, if I do drop him someplace, there's a good chance he's going to ignore the doctor's orders and go walking around without his crutches, which will end up costing me more money, and probably more time.

"Sorry about this." My dad gestures to his foot, his head resting against the window. He sounds anything but sincere.

"Once you're off the crutches, you need to go to a hotel."

"C'mon, kid, this was an accident. You can't be pissed at me 'cause I fell."

I grip the steering wheel. "You can't show up, create all this chaos, and expect me to be okay with it."

"I tried to call; you didn't answer. I just wanted to visit with my son. Where's the crime in that?"

This conversation is pointless. Aside from being on a bunch of medication, my dad's not one to own his mistakes, or be honest. But I'm angry, so instead of keeping my mouth shut, I go ahead and say things I shouldn't—even though all it's going to do is rattle the cage.

"You know, I could deal with it when it was just me in the house, but Lily lives there now, too, so you can't camp out on my couch for three weeks until you pull your shit back together anymore."

"You embarrassed of me? Is that the problem?"

"Yeah, I'm fucking embarrassed. I get home last night from a weekend away, and you're wasted as shit. It wasn't really a great introduction." I hit the brakes when the light turns yellow and piss off the guy behind me because I don't run it.

"I'll apologize to her later. Will that make you feel better?"

"It might if it actually meant something, but you were already into the beers again this morning. You've got a problem, and you need to deal with it."

"Everyone's got problems. That's not a reason to send me to a hotel."

I look at my dad, at the mess he's made of his life. "That's not why you can't stay with us. I don't trust you with her."

"I'm not gonna touch your chippy."

"She's not my fucking chippy, and that's not what I mean. I mean I don't trust you not to be an asshole, or to say something to make her question my loyalty to her. But since you mentioned it, if you lay a fucking finger on her, for any reason, I will kick the motherfucking shit out of you."

He raises his hands in the air in mock surrender. "Whoa, whoa, settle down. I'm not here to mess with you, or this girl you're so hung up on. Just watch your back, kid. They're always after something."

"You mean like Mom? She had such unrealistic expectations

and all, what with wanting you to keep your damn dick in your pants and out of the bunnies. Pretty fucking unreasonable, yeah?" I pull up in front of the house. "You need to get out. I gotta get Lily from work."

He doesn't move for a few seconds, just stares at me. "Randy—"

"Lily's waiting on me, and I don't have time to listen to your bullshit."

He fumbles around with his crutches and opens the door. It takes him a bit to get out, and I don't offer to help.

I roll down the window when he's on the sidewalk. "Try not to get sauced before I get home. It'd be nice if you could keep a handle on your mouth in front of Lily."

I feel a vague sense of vindication at the look of remorse on his face as I take off, but I doubt it will last long. It never does.

It's after seven thirty by the time I arrive at the arena, and Lily's on the ice with Finlay. I knew I wouldn't make it before they got started, so I stopped at a coffee shop, and I even picked up something for him, because I'm trying to be nice. I want to take Lily out after this since I couldn't meet her earlier —and partly to avoid spending any more time with my dad. I also have to break it to her that he's staying a couple more nights with us, and I don't know how she's going to feel about that.

I stay close to the door instead of taking a seat in the stands, so as not to appear like the jealous boyfriend I am. She's so graceful out there. Sometimes I still can't believe she was robbed of her opportunity to be in the Olympics. Whenever I mention it, she reminds me that if she'd gone, we probably never would have met. I don't think I'm better than the Olympics, but Lily always tries to find the positive, and I'm glad I get to be her silver lining.

I wait until the last five minutes of their ice time before I approach the boards. They seem to be mostly done, so I'm not at risk of interrupting. Lily raises her hand in a wave and holds up a finger. I lean against the boards and pretend to look at my phone while I wait.

I have messages from Lance, seeing how I'm dealing with my dad being around. Lance's family relationships are strained, too. Much of his family's still in Scotland, though, so he only sees them once or twice a year. He's aware that things with my dad aren't good, so when Randall, Sr., comes to town, Lance and Miller have a tendency to check on me.

"Hey, you." Lily's skates send up a spray of ice as she stops in front of me.

I look up from my phone. "Hi. I brought you tea, and a coffee for Finlay, if he wants it."

"That's sweet of you. He's already gone to change."

I look around the rink to find it empty.

She leans in with a knowing smile and kisses my cheek. "I saw you skulking by the doors."

"I wasn't skulking. I didn't want to make Finlay nervous. Or seem like a jealous boyfriend."

She arches a brow. "Are you jealous?"

"Mostly I wanted to see you on the ice."

"Mostly?"

"Yeah, mostly. Ninety percent is me wanting to watch you skate; the other ten percent is me being jealous."

She presses a quick kiss to my lips. "I can deal with ten-percent jealousy."

The heavy feeling in my stomach eases up a little. "I was thinking maybe we could go for dinner once you're changed, unless you've eaten."

"I had a snack, but that sounds fantastic. I'm starving."

"Great. I'll meet you in the lobby?"

"Perfect. I'll be quick." Lily skates away, taking her tea with her and leaving Finlay's coffee with me.

I call and make a reservation at Lily's favorite restaurant. It's last-minute, but we go there a lot, so they're able to get me a table.

Finlay comes out of the men's locker room before Lily comes out of the women's. He looks uncertain when he sees me, but I put on my best, least-menacing smile.

"Hey, man, how's it going?" I ask.

"Good. We finished up a while ago. I'm sure Lily will be out soon." He adjusts the strap on his bag.

"Yeah. I saw her already. This is for you." I hold out the coffee.

He looks at it like it's a grenade.

"It's not poisoned or anything. I know I was a dick the last time, so this is, like, a peace offering."

"Oh. Well, thanks."

"Yeah, no problem. You know, just keep it professional out there on the ice, and we're good."

Based on his expression, that may not have come out the way I meant it.

"I'm kidding. I mean, not really, but I'm not going to show up with a crowbar and take out your knees or anything." I close my eyes and expel a breath. "I'd really appreciate it if you didn't tell Lily I said that."

"Tell her what?"

I give him a thumbs up.

"Does it help if I tell you I have a girlfriend?"

"Only if you're not lying."

"I'm not lying."

"That's fuckin' awesome." I slap him on the shoulder and almost knock the coffee cup out of his hand. "Shit. Sorry."

"You're good. Hey, uh, I don't know if this is weird or not, but do you think I can get an autograph? I don't know if Lily told you, but I'm a huge fan."

"Really? Sure, I'm happy to sign something for you."

The awkwardness—or rather, my awkwardness—seems forgotten as he pulls out a puck, a scrapbook, and a silver Sharpie like he's been preparing for this. "If you could sign the puck for me, and the scrapbook belongs to my girlfriend. Her name's Leanne."

Lily comes out of the changing room as I pass the scrapbook and puck back to him. "I can get you tickets to a home game, if you want."

"For real? That'd be amazing."

I tell him I can hook him up for the first home game of the season. He freaks out, thanks me ten times, and then takes off.

Lily waits until he's out of hearing range. "That was really sweet."

"See? I can be nice. Ready for dinner?"

Her stomach rumbles. "So ready."

We leave the arena and cross the street to my truck. Lily tells me funny stories about her little-kid lessons as we drive, but she looks confused when we pull up to the restaurant and the valet opens her door.

"I'm not really dressed for this."

I didn't think about the dress code when I made the reservations. I'm wearing jeans, and she's wearing leggings. I'm in a T-shirt, and she has on a pretty, flowy top. "No one's gonna care, but we can go somewhere else if you're uncomfortable."

She kisses my cheek. "If you don't care, I don't care."

We end up at our favorite table in a private corner at the back of the restaurant, so what we're wearing doesn't matter anyway. I should tell Lily that my dad is staying longer than I'd hoped, but I don't want to ruin a perfectly good evening, so I decide to wait.

Only it doesn't work, because as soon as the waiter's done taking our drink and appetizer order, Lily asks about the trip to the hospital.

"They ended up having to dig more glass out of his foot. He's got something like twenty-five stitches."

"Oh, God."

"Yeah."

"Is he okay?"

"They gave him some pretty sweet painkillers. I'm sure he's fine."

She covers my hand with hers. "Are you okay? You don't seem okay."

"I have to take him back to the doctor in a couple of days. I feel like it's better if I'm watching him, so I told him he could stay with us until then. But after that he's going to a hotel. Are you okay with that?"

"Are you?" Lily's voice is soft, like the tips of her fingers tracing the petals on the back of my hand.

"I'd rather he be gone, but if I don't take care of this, he sure as hell isn't going to, and then it'll be an even bigger mess to clean up."

Lily's bottom lip slides between her teeth as she regards me. "So you're doing this out of obligation."

"I don't want him showing up at my mother's doorstep, looking to stay there."

"That's happened before, I take it?"

"Only once since I moved to Chicago, but I don't want him to try it again."

"I'll support whatever decision you make, and it's fine if you want him to stay with us so you can monitor him. But my biggest concern is how this affects you."

"He'll be gone in a couple of days, and then I won't see him again for another six months—or longer if I'm lucky. I can manage. You're sure you're okay with it?"

Lily nods and slips her fingers under mine. "Like I said, he's your father. I get that you feel some responsibility for managing this situation, but you didn't create it. The important question is, how long will it take for you to be fine once he's gone?"

It's a good question. I don't have an answer for it.

"So I'm guessing we're out for dinner because you're avoiding him?" she asks after a moment.

"And you were hungry."

"Does he know how hard this is on you?"

I shrug. "Doubtful."

"Maybe he needs to be told."

"I've told him. He's not often prepared to listen. I don't think he can see far enough outside of himself to even care."

We don't finish dinner until almost eleven. When we get home, my dad is passed out on the couch. But only two beer bottles sit on the coffee table. Lily heads for the bedroom, stuffed full of food and tired after a long day. I collect the empties and take them to recycle. There seem to be a lot more bottles in there than I remember from this morning. Before I move my dad to the spare room, I check the fridge. There are no beers, and I know for a fact there were half a dozen this morning. This means my dad didn't listen; he just tried to fool me into believing he did.

I leave him on the couch where he is. If I wake him up, I'll fight with him, and I don't have the energy for that.

Lily's already in bed when I get there. She's naked. Willing to be my distraction. Because I need one. Because she loves me. Because I love her enough to let her.

11

ENOUGH
IS ENOUGH

LILY

R andy stays glued to my hip the next morning while I'm in the house. He won't leave me alone with his dad at all. It was easier for both of us that I left early this morning, and drove myself, to teach classes that run most of the day.

Randy's even more tense and agitated now. As much as I want to be the supportive, easy-going girlfriend, I'll be glad when his dad is gone. His presence has totally overshadowed the amazing weekend at the cottage. That already feels like it was a lifetime ago.

I'm distracted during my lessons, checking my phone every chance I get. Randy messages a couple of times to tell me everything is fine, but I'm still worried.

When I return home, Randy's ordered in dinner so I don't

have to cook, which I appreciate since I've been at work all day. I'm also not sure how I'd manage cooking for his dad. Seems like that could go all kinds of wrong. When the Chinese food is delivered, Randall, Sr., isn't thrilled. He complains, yet he still manages to load up his plate.

Conversation is forced and strained as we eat. I'm pretty sure Randy's dad is drunk, which seems to be typical.

"So, Lily—it's Lily right?" At my nod he smiles. "Where's your accent from? I can't place it."

"I'm from outside of Toronto. It's in Ontario, Canada." No one actually knows where Guelph is, but most people have heard of Toronto.

"Really? Canada, *eh*?"

I smile, because it's the polite thing to do when people make fun of how I speak. Under the table I'm flipping him off.

"So you moved to Chicago for this guy?" He points his fork at Randy.

"She moved because she got a great job," Randy says irritably.

"Teaching skating lessons, right? Can't you do that in Canada? Lots of ice up there, right?"

"I could and I did, but there are more opportunities here, and I have friends in the area." This is starting to feel like an inquisition.

"So what happens when Randy gets traded again? You gonna get your own place and stay put in Chicago?"

Randy slaps the table. "Dad."

He lifts a shoulder. "What? Your contract is up with Chicago in two more years. I'm just asking what she's gonna do."

"It's up in three years, not two."

"Yeah, but the way you play sometimes... Anyway, whenever it happens, it's not like you're gonna marry her and take her with you—or is that part of your plan?"

I can tell he's pushing Randy's buttons on purpose.

"We haven't really talked about that since it's so far into the future," I jump in, squeezing Randy's leg under the table.

"Who even knows if you'll still be together by then, right?" His dad shoves a forkful of noodles into his mouth, thankfully shutting his asshole trap.

When he asks me personal questions about my family, Randy redirects the topic to his own sister, who's been in Australia for the past year. She went there for college to get away from their father, I've been told. I don't know if that's a perceived or actual reality. But based on the limited and supervised contact I've had with Randall, Sr., I wouldn't be all that surprised if it was the truth.

"So is Brynne planning to do something with this college diploma she's getting, or is she gonna hook up with a surfer out there and play around for a couple more years?"

And now I'm certain Randy wasn't exaggerating about his sister's exit from the continent.

Randy grits his teeth and pushes his plate away. "I'm done with dinner."

"I'll clean up." I grab his plate and mine.

"Why don't you relax? You haven't even had a shower or anything since you got home." It's Randy's way of asking me to disappear without saying it outright. I don't fight him, but I'm worried about what's going to go down when I leave the room.

I excuse myself to the bedroom, but keep an ear open in case a brawl breaks out in the living room. Randall, Sr., is constantly poking at Randy's insecurities. This glimpse into his family history explains a lot, and it makes me even more appreciative that Randy's allowed me into his life the way he has. I almost offered to stay with Sunny and Miller while his dad's here, but then I'd be leaving Randy alone with his father. I think that's far worse than me being a little uncomfortable for a couple of days.

Randy peeks his head in our room half an hour later. I'm watching mindless TV on the laptop. He closes the door and flips the lock. His expression is hard to read as he climbs into bed. I hold my arms open for him.

He settles his head on my chest and wraps an arm around my waist. "He'll be gone tomorrow before you get home from work."

Tomorrow afternoon Randy has his first team meeting of the new season. I'll get home before him. Next week training camp begins, and that means his free time is going to diminish significantly.

I close the laptop and run my fingers through his hair. "I'm sorry this is so hard for you."

"It's a mind fuck, you know? Like, I see how he is now, and I keep trying to figure out where it all went wrong. I don't want his mistakes to be mine."

"You're already so different than he is. I know we can't predict the future, but we can always learn from the past and try not to fall into the same patterns, right?"

He's silent for a while, just breathing. "I see what you're saying. But I still want him gone so I can have you to myself for the next few days. I hate that he's cutting into my last week with you before training starts."

"Like you said, he'll be gone tomorrow, and we'll have this weekend. I only teach Saturday morning."

"I don't want to share you this weekend, okay?"

"Okay."

"Do you need distractions?"

Randy shakes his head and winds his arms more tightly around me. "I just want this right now. Is that okay?"

I know Randy's stressed when he doesn't want sex. My biggest worries now are how he's going to deal with all these long-buried emotions and what things are going to be like after his dad finally leaves.

I DRIVE myself to the arena again the next morning since Randy's taking his dad to follow up with the doctor and he has his team meeting in the afternoon. I'm on edge all day, mostly because I don't hear from Randy other than a brief message to let me know the doctor's appointment went fine and he'll see me at home.

I don't know what kind of mood he's going to be in tonight—the beginning of the season is always a transition, and this will be the first time I've been through this with him. It's his second season with Chicago, but a lot happened last year, and their rough end to last season means the pressure's on for a better start up.

The house is quiet when I get home. The emptiness is actually welcoming. I head straight to the bedroom. I want to shower and change into something more...interesting. I open my underwear drawer and sift through my panties and bras. I pick out a few options and lay them on the bed. I'm not sure if Randy would prefer something sweet or more sex kitten.

My phone buzzes with a message from him.

> **Home in less than 20.**

I send him a picture of the scraps of lace laid out on the bed.

> **Any preference?**

The humping dots appear right away.

> **Do we still have the red ribbon?**

A shiver runs down my spine. Oh, God. I'm in for it tonight. I rummage through the drawer and find the roll of red satin. I send him a picture of it in response. His next message comes seconds later.

> **Can't fucking wait.**

"Having fun playing house?"

I gasp and drop the ribbon on the floor. Spinning around, I find Randy's dad leaning against the door jamb. He drops his gaze to the bed where all my pretty things are laid out. I hastily gather them and shove them back in the drawer.

"I didn't realize anyone was here. I thought you were staying at a hotel." Randy said he was taking him as far away from us as possible.

"I forgot a couple of things." An unfriendly smile makes his cheek tic. "It's a pretty sweet setup you have going on, isn't it? Living here?"

He sounds so much like Randy. They have the same deep voice, same broad shoulders, same eyes, same mannerisms, but that's where it ends. This man is a version of Randy missing all the good pieces.

I ignore his question. "Does Randy know you're here?"

He shifts so he takes up more of the doorway. I'm suddenly very nervous. He's blocking my only way out of the room. Based on the loose way his eyes move over me, I have to assume he's drunk.

"Come on, sweetheart. You and I both know you're in this for the free ride."

He's been circling this conversation for the past couple of days, making little comments that seem innocuous but aren't. I cross my arms over my chest, mostly so I don't end up slapping him across his smug, jerk face.

"You don't know the first thing about my relationship with Randy."

"I don't need to. I know my son. He's got a short attention span when it comes to women. I would've thought he'd learned by now that this little thing he's got going on isn't gonna work out, but I can see why he'd want to give it a shot, at least for a while. He'll figure out soon enough that you're just using him like everyone else."

"*I'm* using him?" I've about had it with this man. "Jesus. Do you hear yourself talking? You're the most selfish person I've ever met. You show up on his doorstep whenever you damn well feel like it, make yourself at home in his house, eat his food, ask for handouts, and spend your time telling him how he's going to fail."

He opens his mouth to cut me off, and I hold up a hand. "I'm not done yet, so hold your vitriol-fueled shot until I'm damn well finished. You know, most parents want better for their kids, but all you do is drag him down." I motion to his disheveled appearance. "You make him believe that this is what he's destined for. You're everything he's afraid to become, and you send him spinning every time you come back into his life. You don't deserve his generosity or his loyalty. You need to be out before he gets home."

He laughs. "This isn't your house. I don't have to go anywhere."

"Newsflash, asshole, I live here, so I have a say in who gets to stay and who doesn't. Randy needs to focus on getting ready for the season, and all you're doing is sabotaging him by saying he's not good enough."

"Everybody falls sooner or later; he needs to come to terms with that."

"You are such a self-absorbed bastard."

His grin is malicious. "He's exactly like me."

"He's nothing like you." Randy will be home soon. I don't have much time to get his dad gone.

He grabs my wrist as I stalk past him. "That boy is good at two things: hockey and fucking things up. As soon as he's back on the road, he's gonna have access to everything he's been missing out on while he's had you here keeping house for him."

"Just because you screwed up your life doesn't mean he's going to do the same."

The front door opens with a beep and closes with a slam. "Lily, baby? Where you hiding? I'm ready to unwrap you!"

Randy rounds the corner as his dad drops my wrist.

His gaze moves from me, clutching my wrist in the doorway of our bedroom, to his father. "What the hell is going on? Why are you here? I dropped you off at the hotel hours ago."

"Settle down, son. We were just talking."

Randy's eyes are wild. He holds out his hand, and I go to him. "Why were you touching her?"

As soon as I'm within reach, he wraps a protective arm around me. He gently pries my fingers from my wrist and checks the faint red marks from his dad's tight hold. In one swift move, Randy shifts me behind him and closes the distance between him and his father.

"You fucking bastard."

The sound of flesh hitting flesh has me between them before Randy can throw a second punch. I cover his shaking fist. "Baby, these hands are too important. Don't let him ruin your season."

Randy takes a few deep breaths before he points a shaking finger at his father. "I hope you get that she's the only reason you're gonna walk away with teeth. Get the fuck out of this house. Now."

His father picks himself up off the floor. He wipes his lip with the sleeve of his shirt, smearing it with blood, and starts to speak.

"Don't." I put a hand out to stop him. "You've said and done more than enough. Just get out."

He snickers. It's a wet sound. "You're a feisty one, aren't you?"

"You bet your ass I am."

Randy calls a cab, which is good because there's no way I'd let him drive his dad anywhere. Randall, Sr., doesn't get to be alone with him again so he can hammer more shit into his head. While we wait, his dad searches his room for something he never actually finds. I have a feeling he came back to pilfer pawnable items or create more drama.

The look on Randy's face scares me as we walk his dad to the door. It's like he's shut down.

The cab is already waiting. His dad pauses and looks at me. "You think you've changed him, but he is who he is—"

"For Christ's sake, will you shut up? Is this how you make yourself feel better about how empty and shitty your life is? And that's a rhetorical question, so you don't need to waste any more words with a response." I'm about to close the door in his face, when I decide I have a few more for him. "Randy doesn't owe you anything. In fact, you owe him a lifetime of apologies for making him think he's anything less than amazing."

He looks over my head at Randy, so I snap my fingers in his face.

"You look at me, not him. As someone who loves him, it's my responsibility to protect him from people who hurt him when he can't bring himself to do it. As long as I'm in Randy's life, this version of you isn't welcome."

Randy pulls out his wallet and withdraws a stack of bills, reaching around me to tuck them into his dad's shirt pocket. "This should cover you for a few days, until you figure out where you're going and what you're doing. Don't call Mom, and don't call me until you get yourself sorted out."

I step back into the house, close the door, and lock it before either of them can say anything else.

"I was going to change the code when I got home. I didn't think he'd come back." Randy drops his head, his lips finding the place where my neck meets my shoulder. "I should've handled him. You shouldn't have had to do that."

I hate how defeated he sounds. Adrenaline is slamming through my veins, making me hyper-aware and alert. Until Randy came into my life, I never would have had the guts to put someone in their place like that.

"I don't know that he would've had a face left if I'd let you deal with it."

"He put his hands on you."

"He squeezed my wrist; that was all."

"I should never have let him stay here."

"He's your dad, Randy. I get that you want to help him, even though he doesn't deserve it. And you thought he was gone."

"I keep waiting for things to change with him, for him to go back to being someone worth giving a shit about, but it never happens."

Randy seems edgy, fragile, like he did the night I broke things off with him. I inspect his hand. He'll have bruises on his knuckles, but nothing serious.

I bring his fingers to my lips. "Tell me what's going on in your head."

"I hate that he's like this. Why can't he ever just be proud of what I've done? Why does he always have to make me feel like shit?"

I close my eyes for a moment. Randy is a complicated man, but he's intrinsically good, and that's the part his father makes him question. I feel rage boiling and will it back down.

I take his face between my palms so he'll look at me and not his feet. "I'm proud of you."

His smile is sad. "I know. It'd just be nice if he wouldn't crap all over my life every time I see him."

"You're a beautiful man with a beautiful heart. You're all the good things your father isn't. I don't know what happened to him to make him so self-destructive, but I do know at your core you're dramatically different than he is. Maybe he can't handle seeing you become everything he couldn't."

He pulls me into a tight hug. "I don't ever want to lose you."

"I'm not going anywhere."

TWO DAYS after we send Randy's dad packing, he leaves a voicemail on our home phone. It's an apology. He sounds so different that I barely recognize the voice as his. But he also sounds legit, so I return the call, as he requested, and listen to his heartfelt apology in real time. He's going back to Boston, where he's been living for the past year. He's going to dry out and get his life back together. He'll give Randy some space until he does.

I don't tell Randy about the call, because I don't want to give him false hope. I don't know enough about who his father was before his life fell apart to know whether he's capable of putting it back together.

As Randy requested, we blow off our friends for most of the weekend so we can enjoy what's left of our uninterrupted time together. He seems good at the time, but then he's quieter than usual over the next week. Like me, he tends to internalize before he externalizes. Season training begins, taking more time away from us. This continues to fuel his anxiety, but he channels his energy into hockey, leaving me feeling lost.

I spend more time with Sunny, because she's in the same position I am—sort of. She and Miller were together when season training began last year, but she still lived in Canada, not with him, so it was a lot different than it is now. And she wasn't pregnant. Like me, she's gotten used to having her boyfriend around all the time. The sudden shift is jarring. I'm trying not to be too needy.

It's Sunday afternoon. The guys have a practice, and we're sitting in her living room, sifting through the pile of Polaroids from the cottage trip. (I removed several from the stack before it was made available for public viewing.) Sunny's cross-legged on a pillow on the floor with Titan and Andy curled up beside her. Wiener is resting in my lap, which seems to be his new favorite place to hang out. He's supposed to be adopted next week, which makes me sad. I've gotten attached to his wiener-y self.

While the guys are immersed in pre-season training drills and games, we decided to put together photo albums with the pictures we took that weekend. It's way more work than I expected, but it's fun, and it takes my mind off of things. I can tell when Randy had the camera. The focus is always on me.

Sunny groans and puts a hand on her belly. "He's so active. It's like he's doing somersaults in there. Come feel."

I move a disgruntled Wiener from my lap and scoot over to her on the floor, putting a hand on her belly. She lifts her top and moves my hand up. I stay still and wait until I feel the bump and then see the distinct outline of a limb, or something, move across her belly.

"That's incredible. Do you think maybe he'll come early?"

"Fingers crossed."

The baby is due on the first official game day of the season, which is eight days away, and for which the team will not be in Chicago. Sunny's biggest worry is that Miller will be halfway across the country when she goes into labor, and he'll miss the birth. She has a home birth scheduled, with a midwife and everything. If Miller's not around, I'll be the one by her side when she delivers—and of course her mom is planning to come down the week before the baby's due, just in case. Still, Sunny gets emotional at the thought of Miller not being here.

The front door opens, and Miller comes in, followed by Randy. Randy immediately pauses and surveys the scene: my cheek pressed up against Sunny's bare tummy.

"Is someone moving around in there?" Miller kicks off his

shoes and drops to his knees beside Sunny, scaring a sleeping Titan. She jumps out of the way and barks once. Miller puts his hand on Sunny's belly and starts talking to her stomach.

They're so cute. I look over to Randy. His hands are shoved in his pockets. He regards Miller and Sunny with an expression that's the opposite of mine. He looks worried. When he catches me watching him, he gives me a small smile.

Things have been difficult since his dad left, as I figured they would be. The aftermath of Randall, Sr.'s, visit feels like a relationship setback and—compounded with the beginning-of-season jitters and his best friend becoming a father—has made things strained between us. No longer manifesting as possessiveness, Randy's stress now means sex has been less frequent. He's been pulling the tired card the past few days. I fully expect him to pull it tonight.

"Man, you gotta come feel this. It's like a dance party in there." Miller motions Randy over.

"Uhh...I'm good."

Wiener waddles over to Randy and jumps up on his leg. He crouches and gives him a pat on the head, probably happy to have the distraction. After a minute of scratches, Randy makes a big show of stretching.

"You ready to go, luscious?"

"Sure. Let me just clean this up." I motion to the mess on the floor.

Sunny waves me off. "Leave it. I'll be back at it tomorrow afternoon anyway. Oh, and the next time you're over, maybe we can pick your dress for the wedding."

"Isn't that, like, a year away?" I ask.

"My mom wants everything ordered as soon as possible." She's all smiles about this. Wedding preparations for Sunny and Miller are drastically different than they were for her brother. She's letting the mothers take charge and enjoying the process.

"Right, yeah. You can never be too prepared."

"She's already looking into little tuxes for this one." Sunny pats her belly.

I gather my purse and use Randy's chest for balance as I put my shoes on. He helps me into the truck as usual, but doesn't cop a feel or anything. My stomach starts to knot as we head home in silence.

"Was practice okay?"

"Yeah." He glances at me out of the corner of his eye. "It was fine."

After another endless minute of silence I try again. "Is everything okay?"

"Huh?" He turns the radio down.

"You're really quiet."

He runs a hand through his hair. "Sorry. I've got a lot on my mind."

I shove my hands between my thighs. I don't know how to read his mood. This is harder than I thought it would be. "Oh. Okay."

"My dad called today."

"Oh? What did he say?" He promised he wouldn't call Randy until he had himself sorted out.

"I didn't talk to him. He left a message wishing me luck on the start of the season."

"That's good, isn't it?"

"I guess. Yeah." He's quiet for the rest of the ride. He cuts the engine when we pull into the driveway, but doesn't make a move to get out of the truck.

"Randy?" I touch his shoulder.

He turns to look at me, his thumb at his mouth. "I think we need to talk."

My stomach plummets from my throat to the floor, like we've dropped from the summit of a roller coaster. My body immediately feels numb, and my eyes well. All his tension makes sense now—the lack of sex, the quietness.

I raise my hand to my mouth as if that's going to stop the

question I have to ask. "Oh my God. Are you breaking up with me?"

I can't get enough air. Mentally, I consider my options. I can stay with Sunny and Miller until the baby comes, but then what?

Randy's brow furrows. "What?"

"You're breaking up with me." My tears spill over and land in my lap.

"What? No, no, no." He releases his seatbelt, pushes the center console up—heedless of his phone and the change that spills all over the backseat—and slides over. Taking my face in his palms he kisses me, once, twice, a third time. "Shit, Lily, why would you think that?"

I hold on to his wrists and try to take a deep breath, but I can't because now I'm really crying.

I seriously hate crying. So much.

I've been holding on to all this emotional stuff since his dad left, and now here it is.

"I don't know. You said we needed to talk, and we're in the truck, and you've been all quiet, and you haven't really wanted me lately, a–and—" I suck in one of those horrible pitchy breaths. Shit. I'm losing it. It's so girly.

"I don't want you?"

"You said you were tired last night. And the night before that, and two days before that."

"I thought you were just being nice, like you were trying to make me feel better."

"I haven't wanted to push you, so I left it alone."

"Ah, fuck." He presses his lips to my forehead. "I haven't dealt with this very well, have I?"

"I know you're stressed about the beginning of the season," I whisper.

He fingers the ends of my hair. "I am. It's more than that, though."

I wait, because of course there's more. He just has to figure out how to say it.

"I'm worried I can't give you everything you deserve."

I pull away so I can see his face. "What do you mean?"

His honey eyes are pained as he takes my hand in his, playing with my fingers. "I don't know if I can give you what Miller and Sunny have, or Alex and Violet."

"Whoa. That's a big leap from our current situation. Why would you think that's something I'm looking for, especially now?"

Randy shrugs. "Well, that's kinda how this works, right? Like, you moved in with me, and eventually I'll put a ring on your finger, and then we'll do the family thing."

"The family thing?"

Randy blows out a breath. "Like, have kids and stuff."

"This is because of Sunny?"

"I don't know. I guess?" He runs his hands over his thighs. "I mean, with Vi and Alex getting hitched, and now you and Sunny are up to your tits in wedding dress magazines, and there's all this baby stuff, and then my dad showed up—"

"It freaked you out?"

He drops his head and nods, peeking up at me from under his lashes.

"Can I be honest with you?" I ask.

"Yeah. Of course."

"It freaked me out, too."

"Really? But you're so into this stuff with Sunny."

I pat his cheek. God, I love him. "That's because it's not my monkey or my circus. I get to do all the fun stuff, and it's not my show. Sunny's so happy and excited, and I'm happy and excited for her. But that doesn't mean I want the same thing. I'm very content to be her maid of honor and Aunt Lily." I lace our fingers together. "I hope I haven't given you the impression that what they have is what I want."

"Well, no, but you'll want that eventually, right? What if I can't do it?"

"Honestly, Randy, I have no idea what I'm going to want in

the future. I do know that getting married doesn't actually change how two people function in a relationship. Alex and Violet are still weirdos. As for the family thing, I'm only twenty-three. You're only twenty-five. I have no desire to jump on the baby train with Sunny. I'm more than happy to have that experience from the outside right now."

I pause for a second to gather myself. I'm relieved that this isn't the discussion I thought it was going to be. "My mom and I struggled a lot financially when I was a kid. We made it through, but at times it sure wasn't easy being the two of us. I want to make sure I don't end up in a situation like that again, for any reason. You and I have years to figure things out, and those are decisions we'll make together, when it's time to make them. Maybe we'll get married, maybe we won't. We'll see if we want kids at some point. Relationships are about sacrifice and compromise. Sometimes, to have the person you want, you have to give up ideals that are important only because society tells us they are. Does that make sense?"

"Yeah, I think so."

"Good." I put my hands on his shoulders and straddle his lap. "I love you."

His smile is soft. "I love you, too. Sometimes I don't know how to deal with it. I don't want to be away from you when the season starts. Thinking about it makes me edgy."

"Same."

He smiles. "Why do we always have our important conversations in this truck?"

"The same reason we always end up having sex in bathrooms, I guess."

He chuckles at that, but his eyes burn.

I kiss him, because those are all the words we need right now, and because I'm so thankful to see that heat.

RIBBONS

RANDY

Tomorrow is our last pre-season exhibition game. Training is going well. We have two new guys on the team: one's a rookie they've moved up from the farm team, and one's a trade from Philly. They're both good players, and once they get used to the way we play, they'll gel with us just fine.

In the locker room, Lance pulls a shirt over his head while I pack my duffle. "You coming out for a bit?" he asks.

In less than a week I'll be on the road again to start the season. I want to go home to Lily, because my time with her is already running short, but it's also important for me to spend time with my team off the ice. She knows this. I know this. It doesn't make it easier, though.

"I'm going for one beer," Miller says.

"I can do the same."

Miller gets the battle in a way Lance doesn't. Miller's kid is actually due on the day of our first game, which is away. It kind of fucking sucks for him. We're all hoping the kid either decides to make an early entrance or wants to stay in there a little longer, so one way or the other, his dad's in Chicago for the big moment. As much as I'm not interested in joining the baby brigade anytime soon, I sure wouldn't want to miss the occasion if Lily was in the same predicament. Which she isn't. Thank fuck.

When we get to the bar, I message Lily to let her know I'm out with the guys for a bit. In response I get a smiley face and a thumbs up. She's good about this kind of thing. I order a pint of beer and talk strategy with my teammates. Like usual, there are bunnies, but social media has made it pretty clear that I'm not on the market, so they leave me alone for the most part.

Waters is the first to leave, which I find odd because he's the team captain and all, but maybe he's got things going on at home I don't know about.

About an hour into my time at the bar, I get a picture of our bedspread covered with clothes. Actually, it's covered with bras and underwear. I'm pretty sure it's Lily's way of saying I should think about coming home soon.

Twenty minutes later, I get another picture. I hide my phone under the table, half expecting it to be Lily dressed up in one of her matching bra and undie sets. It's not. This time it's that roll of red ribbon. I'm instantly hard. Harder than I would be if she'd sent me a semi-nude picture.

My response is brief and to the point:

Leaving now. Home in 15.

Hers is just as succinct:

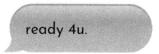

ready 4u.

I leave my beer, say a quick round of goodbyes, and hop in my truck. I don't drive the speed limit home. I don't even try, actually. I run two stale yellows and almost forget to put the truck in park before I get out. I fumble with the lock code—I'm still getting used to the new one—throw open the door, and there she is.

"Holy mother," I groan as I take in the sight before me. I'm quick to step inside and close the door, so no one accidentally gets a glimpse of my gift-wrapped girlfriend. This isn't like the time she answered the door with a bow around her neck. She has that now, too, but this is so, so much better.

She's made quite an effort this time. A thick band of ribbon winds across her chest, covering her nipples. Another piece is threaded between her thighs, somehow attached to the one wrapped around her chest, and all tied up with a pretty red bow in the center. Another wide piece of ribbon is wrapped around her throat with a second bow, and there are also bows on either hip.

Lily fingers the ribbon at her neck. "Did you know we missed an important anniversary earlier this month?"

I mentally scroll through all our important dates. I'm usually good with this kind of thing. Her birthday is in the spring, so I haven't missed it. Mine is December, so it's still a ways off. We officially started dating in January, and the first time I gave her an orgasm was in August, at Waters' Ontario cottage.

She takes a slow step toward me. She's wearing heels. She almost never wears heels. And she has lipstick on. It's red to match the bow. "Want a hint?"

I nod. I don't think I actually have words right now.

"What happened in September last year?" She grabs my belt buckle and pulls it from the clasp.

"September of last year?"

She pops the button on my pants. The way she's biting her lip and palming me through my pants makes it hard to think.

"There was a party…" She drags the zipper down. "You were wearing these underwear, too. Except they were in much better shape then. There's a hole here; did you know that?"

"Huh?" I'm too busy thinking about all the ways I'm going to make her come, and how I want to hook my fingers under that ribbon around her throat and hold onto it while I fuck orgasms out of her. I seriously don't know why it winds me up the way it does.

She sticks her pinkie in the tiny hole near the fly flap, drawing my attention back down to her hand on my crotch.

"Hey! Don't do that. You'll make it bigger." I pin her wrists to her sides.

"Did your teammates see these?"

"So what if they did? They don't care how big my dick is."

Lily giggles. "I guess you have a point. But these are probably ready for the trash."

"They're my favorite."

"I thought I was your favorite."

"You're my favorite person; these are my favorite ball huggers."

"I see."

I lean in for a kiss. I'm not sure what the red lipstick is about; once we get started, it's going to end up smeared all over her face. And mine. I'm actually fine with that.

She turns her head to the side, giving me her cheek. "You still haven't guessed what we're celebrating. You don't get to unwrap me until you do."

"Oh, no?" I kiss along the edge of ribbon at her throat. "I better guess right then, huh?"

She bats her lashes. "You'll get to pull a bow if you do."

"Wow. That sounds pretty damn awesome. So last September…" I let go of her hands and slip a finger under the ribbon running vertically down her torso. I stop just above her pussy. "…was Waters' engagement party." I reverse my path, then trace the edge of the ribbon from the center to the right, and back the other way. Lily shivers. "That was the first time I ever got inside you."

"It was."

I kiss her shoulder. "I wanted to take you back to my place and keep you all weekend."

She angles her head to the side, and I follow the ribbon all the way to her neck. "I wanted that, too."

"I was already way more into you than I should've been for something that was supposed to be all casual."

She runs her fingers through my hair. "I remember thinking it was a good thing you couldn't take me out for dinner."

I back up so I can see her face. "Why was that?"

"Because it would've felt like a date, and I knew it wasn't supposed to be." Lily fingers the hem of my shirt and pulls it over my head.

"I was so fucking stupid."

"Not stupid. Maybe a little clueless, but then so was I." She kisses the center of my chest, leaving a red lip print.

Lily pushes, and I take a step back, then another, and I hit the wall behind me. She drops into a crouch, her face level with my crotch. Her grin is wicked as she pulls my pants and boxer briefs over my hips, setting my dick free. She kisses the tip, leaving another red lip print. Without using her hands, she kisses her way down the shaft.

And now I get why the red lipstick—every kiss leaves another print. When I pull my phone out and quirk a brow in question, Lily grins.

"I can get the digital camera if you'd prefer." She's mostly forgiven me for the lost-phone scare.

"We're good."

She licks the tip when I snap the first pic, and then engulfs the head. She doesn't touch me with anything but her mouth, which drives me fucking crazy. When I warn her I'm about to come, she takes me deeper and keeps her eyes on mine.

When she's done, her lipstick has worn off, and her lips are puffy. I help her up, and she takes my hand, leading me to our bedroom, which is a really great idea. There's a good chance I'm going to fuck fifty damn orgasms out of her tonight, and a bed is the safest, least potentially bruising place for that to go down.

Lily crawls up on the mattress with her ass in the air. Her little ribbon thong panties are fucking obscene with the way the red fabric disappears between her lips. I bet it's rubbing on her clit. I bet she's halfway to coming already. I climb up after her and flip her onto her back, kneeling between her legs.

The ribbon bra is first to go. I pull the bow and watch the red satin fall away. Kissing each nipple, I sit back and appreciate this gift of a woman. The remaining thick band of red hides her clit. I trace the damp edges of the ribbon with my thumbs, and Lily's breath hitches.

I slip two fingers under, tugging it gently upward. She spreads her legs wider and lifts her hips, pulling the ribbon tighter so it rubs right where it should. I tease her like that, using the friction of the satin to get her where I want her: close but not quite there. I drop my head and kiss above her pelvis. When she moans my name, I shift the ribbon to the side so her swollen clit peeks out. I give it a soft lick, and that's all it takes to make her come.

I spend a few more minutes with my face between her thighs, using the ribbon and my tongue to get her off. When I can't wait any longer, I pull the bows on either hip, letting the ribbons fall away. I move her to sit in my lap, easing her onto my cock.

I don't start with vigorous pounding right away. Instead I let Lily roll her hips while I kiss along the edge of the ribbon still tied around her neck.

"I don't know why I love this so fucking much," I mutter against her skin. I really don't have an explanation. I move one hand to the center of her back and splay the other across her sternum. My index finger slips under the ribbon. "I'm leaving this one on."

Lily grins. "I figured as much."

I kiss her one more time. Then I adjust the ribbon so the bow is on the side and slide three fingers under the red satin, curling my fist around it. Lily's throat bobs with a swallow under my knuckles. I caress the line of her jaw with my thumb. "Is this okay?"

Her eyes flutter, and she makes a noise. For a second I think maybe I'm holding on too tight. I start to loosen my grip, but she covers my hand with hers. Then she shudders, and I feel her clench around my cock.

"You coming for me, luscious?"

"Uh-huh."

I brush my lips over hers. "I haven't even started fucking you yet."

"That was my anticipation orgasm. Maybe *I* need to get things started so I can have more."

"I'm gonna say answering the door dressed as a party favor counts as getting things started, but I'm all for more orgasms."

She rests her palm on the side of my neck as she rises up, and then lowers herself slowly. She starts an easy rhythm, and I let her take control—at least at first, because watching her ride me is damn well fantastic. While she moves, Lily rubs her clit, shuddering as another orgasms rolls through her. When she falters, I let go of the ribbon and hold on to her hips.

Eventually I lay her down and reach across to the nightstand for the Polaroid. I take a picture of her orgasm-flushed face and the sexy bow decorating her throat. Then I cover her body with mine, pushing my thumb under the red satin, and cradle the back of her head while she wraps her legs around my waist.

When I come, I keep my eyes on hers, like I did the first time, like I do every time.

I trace the edge of the ribbon. "I know why I like this so much."

"Because you're a kinky fucker?" Lily asks. She's still breathless.

"You think I'm kinky?"

"We get off on getting it on in public bathrooms, and we make sex videos."

"That's a valid assessment."

"I'd still like to hear your hypothesis on why you like the ribbon so much, though." She runs her fingers through my beard.

"I like the idea that you consider yourself a gift."

She makes a face. "Wow. That makes me seem like a narcissist."

"No, it doesn't. You are a gift, Lily. I'm lucky to love you."

"I feel exactly the same way about you." She pulls me down for a kiss. "Maybe next time you should wear the bow."

"Not in a million fucking years."

"Why not?"

"Ribbon necklaces aren't my style." I roll to the side so I'm not at risk of crushing her and pull the blankets up so she doesn't get cold.

"What about moody dick? Of all the presents you give me, he's my favorite to unwrap."

"Still no." I pull the bow at her throat, letting it unfurl and fall away. I kiss the faint line left behind from the tension of me holding it.

Lily lifts her chin so I have better access to her neck. "I thought we were going to sleep."

"We are. Eventually. Unless you need sleep now."

"No, your loving always beats sleep, even if it means you have to wake me up."

"Maybe I'll let you fall asleep, just so I can wake you up."

Lily runs her hand down my chest. "Want me to pretend for you?"

EPILOGUE

NEW ADDITIONS

LILY

TWO WEEKS LATER

The incessant ringing of my cell phone forces my eyes open. I feel for it on the nightstand and groan when I see the time. It's barely six in the morning. I grunt instead of saying hello.

"Lily? Is that you?"

It's Sunny. I make an affirmative noise.

"It's happening."

"Huh?"

"The baby, he's on his way."

I bolt upright. "Oh my God! Oh my God! Where are you? Is Miller there?"

"I'm at home, and the midwife is on her way. Miller's right here with me."

"Oh my God, you're going to be a mom, and I'm going to be an aunt! This is so exciting. What do you need me to do?"

"It's too early for loud." Randy groans and rolls over. Wrapping his arms around my waist, he nuzzles into my lap, his face conveniently close to my Vagina Emporium.

"Nothing right now. Titan and Andy might need to be walked in a bit, but Miller can probably do that." His disapproval over this plan comes through loud and clear in the background. "Or maybe you can stop by and take them for a walk. Um, Wiener might be an issue, though."

Randy mumbles something about wieners and curls himself around me even more. He's pretty much head-butting my vagina.

"Is Wiener okay?"

"He's anxious. He hasn't stopped barking for the last hour. I wondered if maybe you could take him for a couple of days— just until we get things settled here with the baby? He loves Randy, and you, so..."

"Of course! We'd love to have him. When should I come get him? Like, now?"

"Whenever is fine. Oh! Hold on! Contraction." Sunny makes a sound like she's uncomfortable. It's followed by some labored breathing. "It looks like they're getting closer together. I should probably go. I'll have Miller call as soon as the baby's born if you don't stop by to pick up Wiener before it happens!"

"Okay. Good luck!"

I hang up the phone and try to disengage myself from Randy, but he wraps himself around me and keeps on head-butting me in the vag.

"I need to get dressed. Miller and Sunny are having the baby!"

He lifts his head. His hair is a mess, and his beard is just as unruly. "Huh?"

"Sunny's finally in labor."

He blinks at me a few times. "No shit. Good thing he decided to come before the next away series."

"I'm sure she's relieved."

Randy nods, still bleary-eyed and half asleep. "Oh, man. We do have a game tonight, though. I wonder if Miller's gonna make it."

"I can't believe you're worried about the game! You are such a boy!" I try to disentangle my legs from his arms, but he grabs me behind the knees and pulls me down so he can lie on top of me. He rubs his morning wood, which is confined by nothing, on my underwear-covered vagina.

"That probably feels more man than boy, don't you think?"

"I don't have time for sex, and you're being an insensitive jerk, so even if I did have time, my vagina isn't interested."

Randy nuzzles my neck. "I'm kidding about the game, and you don't need to rush. It's not like you being there is going to make it happen any faster."

"You're just saying that so you can get inside the Vagina Emporium."

"I think a trip to the Vagina Emporium is necessary on a day like today."

"Oh? And why's that?"

"Other than it being a game day, I feel it's important for us to take advantage of the fact that we can have sex whenever we feel like it. Miller and Sunny definitely aren't going to be able to do that for a long while."

"So this is sympathy sex?"

"Exactly. Sympathy sex." He uses the head of his cock to nudge my panties out of the way.

"You're a real—"

"Shh." Randy puts his finger against my lips, eyes wide and darting around the room. "Do you hear that?"

"What?" I listen, but I don't hear a thing.

"You can't hear it?"

"Hear what?"

He lowers his mouth to my ear. "It's the sound of my cock calling for your pussy."

I slap his ass when he laughs. Then we both groan, and I dig my fingernails into his ass cheeks as he sinks into me.

FORTY-FIVE MINUTES later we're showered, dressed, and on the way to Miller and Sunny's house. Randy brought the Polaroid camera—and a present he bought for the baby a while back but hasn't shown me, because he didn't trust me not to blab it to Sunny. I'd be offended, but if it's cute, he has a point.

"Should we stop for coffee? Do you think Miller will want one?" Randy asks.

"I have no idea. We could get him one in case he does?"

We stop at Starbucks and get Sunny a ginger lemon ice tea, and I get myself a mint one. Randy orders coffee for himself and Miller. By the time we get to the house, it's after eight-thirty. Randy texts Miller, and I go to the fence to say hi to the dogs, who are super excited to see us.

Randy doesn't hear anything back after a few minutes, so we decide it's best to take the dogs for a walk while we wait. I let Randy take Andy, because he weighs more than I do, and I take Titan and Wiener. He was supposed to be adopted by now, but it fell through. I'm not all that sad because he's fantastic. We spend a good hour at the dog park a few blocks away, where they can roam around and sniff each other's butts. Wiener stays pretty close, sitting on Randy's foot half the time. Then he jumps up and puts his paws on Randy's knee, like he's looking to get on the bench with us. Randy picks him up, and he settles beside him, his little chin propped on Randy's thigh.

"You are just the cutest!" I give his head a scratch. "And so are you." I scratch under Randy's beard and give him a quick kiss on the lips.

"I always wanted a dog as a kid," he says.

"Why didn't you get one?"

"Too many away games and competitions. We would've had to kennel a dog a lot when games were out of town. It wouldn't have been fair."

"I never had a dog, but Sunny always did, so it was kind of like they were mine, too."

We get a group text on our way back to Miller and Sunny's place:

> Welcome Logan Waters
> Butterson, born at 8:44 am,
> October 13th, 8lbs 13oz.

The message is followed by a picture of Sunny holding the tiny little bundle.

The first person to reply is Violet.

> Congratulations! My beaver is
> crying for your beaver.

A slew of new messages make our phones go off incessantly all the way back to their house. We put the dogs back in the yard and knock on the door. A rental car is parked out front, so I'm assuming Daisy's here, and possibly Skye as well.

Miller lets us in, and Sunny's lying on the couch, wrapped in her favorite blankets with a green bundle cradled in her arms. She's beaming. She looks beautiful and tired. If there's anyone who will be good at this mom thing, it's Sunny. She's so calm about life, and about how things work out even when they're unexpected.

I hug Miller, whose smile mirrors Sunny's, and then go meet my new surrogate nephew. He's a tiny miracle. Randy checks the little guy out and gives Sunny the small gift bag he had professionally wrapped.

"Do you want to hold him while I open it," she asks.

"What? Uh, no!" Randy holds his hands up like he's being robbed at gunpoint with a nuclear weapon. "I mean, Lily will probably want to hold him. He's like, brand new. I don't think it's a good idea."

Of course I want to hold him, but I want to see Randy hold him almost as much. I'll get my turn soon enough.

"You'll be fine. Just hold your arms like me," Sunny says.

Randy sits down on the couch beside her and mimics Sunny's position so she can transfer Logan into the generous space.

"If you're not comfortable, I can hold him." Miller extends his arms, glancing nervously at Randy. It's sweet.

"He'll be fine, Miller." She eases a snuffling Logan into his arms.

"What do I do now?"

"You hold him exactly as you are. He's tired from all the work we just did, so he's pretty sleepy."

Randy's stiff as he cradles Logan, obviously unsure and uncomfortable. It's endearing. He looks up at me. "He's so tiny."

"He is. It's a good thing, too, considering where he came from."

"I can't get over how small he is," Randy muses.

Daisy and Skye come out of the kitchen at the sound of Randy's voice. They *ooh* and *aah* over how sweet he looks holding Logan. It's the first time I've ever seen him blush.

I snap a couple of pictures with the Polaroid while Sunny opens the gift. Inside is a tiny jersey with the team logo. On the back is Butterson 04, just like his dad's.

"It's probably too big right now," Randy says.

"It'll be perfect in a few months. Thank you."

"You're welcome. Can I give him back now?"

Sunny laughs and looks to me. "Do you want to hold him?"

"Of course." I take my turn, slipping my pinkie finger under Logan's tiny hand. I think about all the changes to Sunny's life now that he's here, how different it will be, how things will never be the same, and how she's okay with that. I consider how this will change her relationship with Miller; it's not just about them anymore. Their number one has changed. Logan will be the most important person in their lives now.

I'm happy to have Randy as my number one, and I'm happy to be his.

People start showing up not long after this. Violet and Alex and both of their dads—now grandpas—with Charlene and Darren. We hang out for a short while, then move to the back-yard to entertain the dogs. Around lunchtime, Randy and I gather Wiener's toys and take him back to our place.

Randy's quiet on the ride home.

"You okay?"

"Yeah, I'm fine." He stretches his arm across the backseat and threads his fingers through the hair at the nape of my neck. Wiener's curled up alongside his leg. He'd be in Randy's lap if he wasn't driving.

"A little overwhelmed?"

"I've never held a baby that new or that small before."

"Me either."

He's silent again for the rest of the trip. I don't push him to talk, because sometimes words aren't going to make a difference. He parks the truck in the driveway and taps the wheel for a few seconds while staring at me.

"Do you want to go in?" I ask.

"Right. Yeah."

We bring all of Wiener's toys inside. His favorite, ironically, is a stuffed hot dog. He follows Randy around the house with it in his mouth. He's freaking adorable.

"Come hang out with me." Randy pats the cushion next to him on the couch. Wiener jumps up and takes the space before I can, but Randy moves him to the other side so I can snuggle in with him. "Is it wrong that I'm glad I don't have to share you like Miller's gonna have to share Sunny now?"

I shift so I can look at him. "You mean her attention?"

"Yeah, I guess, but it's more than that. He's gonna have to share her love, too. I don't think I'd like that."

"You don't think her heart has enough room for both of them?"

"No. I mean, yeah, of course she has enough room. I'm not saying this right. That baby changes everything, and he's gonna take time away from them. I'm already gone half the year. I don't think I'd want to come home after being away for a week and have to share you with someone else. Wow, that makes me a selfish asshole, doesn't it?"

"I think it makes you human. I've thought the same thing. I've also thought about how hard it's going to be for Miller to be away from both of them."

"Babies are some scary shit."

"That's why my vote is on dogs. I'd say cats, because they're easier, but I'm allergic, so they're out. We could always talk to Sunny about keeping Wiener if we like having him. She told me his other adoption fell through."

"I like that idea." Randy traces the line of my shin. "I'm not saying I'd never want that with you, though—a family, I mean. I think one day, like, a long time in the future, it would be okay."

"You don't have to explain. I get exactly what you mean. I like what we have right now. I don't want to change it."

"How are you so perfect?" Randy palms the back of my neck and gives me a soft, lingering kiss.

I think this means the end of this conversation for now,

except he bends me forward. It's an awkward position. My nose hits my knees.

"What're you doing?"

"Checking for your drone microchip." His lips touch the top of my spine.

I'm not exactly in a position designed for retaliation, but I manage to get an arm free so I can pinch him. He releases the back of my neck, and I pop up, but before I can launch a counter-attack, he lays me out on the couch. Wiener jumps down and barks twice before running around in a circle.

"Sorry, buddy," Randy says over his shoulder, then turns back to me. "No microchip. You're one-hundred-percent real, and you're all mine."

Wiener paces beside the couch, then puts his paws up beside our heads and whines.

"Well, maybe not *all* yours. I think you have to share me with Wiener now."

Randy runs his palm up the outside of my thigh and rolls his hips. "I have another wiener that wants a piece of you."

I snicker. "You're ridiculous."

"That I am. I'm pretty sure that's why you love me."

"It's one of many reasons."

His smile is beautiful, just like the rest of him.

There is no end to my love for this man. Randy's my happily ever after, and I'm his.

Read on for a preview of Pucked Off

BONUS EPILOGUE

ONLY YOU

RANDY

"Look at my big, beautiful Wiener. You're the handsomest Wiener I've ever seen. Yes you are!"

I round the corner, ready to tell my girlfriend that the big, not-so-beautiful wiener in my pants is jealous about the attention our pet dog is getting, but I stop short when I see what's going on in our living room.

Crouching around Wiener is my girlfriend Lily, and several of my teammates other halves including Lily's half-sister Violet, Charlene, Sunny, Poppy and Lainey—my teammate Rook's baby mama.

They all look positively gleeful, which isn't unusual when those women get together. But what is highly unusual is the forlorn look on my poor dog's face. Normally he loves all the

163

attention he gets when the girls come over and hang out, but not today.

Because they've dressed him up.

In a little tux and party hat.

His sad brown eyes meet mine from across the room and I can pretty much see the humiliation written on his traumatized dog-face.

I slip my hand out of the front of my sweats, mentally tell my dick we'll have to take a rain check—neither of us is excited about this prospect—and clear my throat to signal my presence.

"What's going on here?" Translation: *why are you torturing my dog?*

"Oh! I didn't realize you were home!" Lily pops to her feet like a sprung jack-in-the-box. Instead of skirting around the coffee table, she hops lithely up and launches herself gracefully into the air.

I catch her around the waist and she loops her arms around my neck, letting me hold her a good eight inches off the floor so our faces remain level with each other. "Just got back." I had a list a mile long of things I was supposed to pick up for the party we're throwing here tonight. It's Lily's birthday, and she wanted a low-key get together, which loosely translates into all of our friends coming over and getting sauced.

Lily's gaze roams my face and the moment her dark choco-late eyes lock with mine, me and my dick forget all about the fact that we're not alone.

Until Wiener lets out a small, forlorn bark.

It breaks the thick sexual tension—sort of—and Lily glances over her shoulder. I reluctantly tear my eyes away from my girl-friend's face to find everyone staring at us.

"You two need ten minutes in the bathroom?" Violet quips.

Lily rolls her eyes. "He'll survive."

I kiss the side of her neck, feeling the heavy thud of her pulse under my lips and allow her to slide down the front of my body.

"That's questionable since my balls are already turning blue," I mutter.

Lainey, who's the newest addition to the crew, blushes and looks away, rubbing the back of her neck the way people tend to do when our PDA's get a little much. Which admittedly is probably often. Also, I'm not sure I said that part about my balls all that quietly.

It doesn't matter how long Lily and I have been together, nothing really tempers our appetite for each other. And we've been together for a long time. The longest I've ever been with anyone, actually. Although, by the time we'd reached the three-month mark, Lily had officially become my longest relationship.

Lily pats me on the chest and gives me a saucy grin that promises the wait will be worth it, which is pretty much the only reason I don't drag her down the hall to the bathroom and bend her over the vanity. Also, I recognize that I should show some restraint every once in a while, and I don't want to make Lainey so uncomfortable that she won't come back here again.

"Wanna tell me why my dog is dressed up like a drunk butler?" I motion to Wiener, who hasn't dropped the forlorn look at all.

"Violet made him a birthday outfit," Lily explains.

I cock an eyebrow at my girlfriend's half-sister. "Emasculating Alex's dick isn't enough for you anymore, you need to torture my dog, too?"

"Superhero costumes aren't emasculating, they're badass, and Wiener looks adorable. We already posted a pic on his Instagram account and it has over a thousand likes." She holds out her phone so I can see the picture of my poor, sad dog. The post does, in fact, have more than a thousand likes already and it's only been up for twenty minutes. Lily set Wiener up with his own account, which actually has almost as many followers as I do.

People love cute dogs almost as much as they love hockey players, apparently.

"Why does my dog need a birthday outfit?"

"Because it's cute," Violet says, "And because I'm giving you the gift of motivation." She gives me a meaningful look I don't understand.

I don't have a chance to find out what the hell I need motivation for because five phones chime simultaneously from various points in the room.

"Oh! Time to go!" All of a sudden there's a flurry of action. Violet and Lily undress Wiener together.

"Go?" I lean against the wall and jam a hand in my pocket.

"We have hair and make up appointments, remember?" Lily reminds me.

"Right, yeah." I didn't remember at all, to be honest. Lily's always gorgeous and my brain is still focused on how soon I can get her naked. "How long are you gonna be gone?"

"A few hours."

Poppy crosses over to the playpen that's been set up in the corner of the room. She lifts Quinn out and smothers his face in kisses before she turns to me. "Lance and Miller should be here in about half an hour, you'll be okay with Quinn until then." It's phrased more as a statement than a question.

"Uh . . ." she holds him out to me and I have no option but to take him. "Sure?"

Aside from Charlene and Darren, Lily and I are the only other ones in our friend group who don't have kids. We have Wiener, which is sort of the same, sort of not. He requires care and love like a kid, but not to the same degree.

Quinn's shock of red hair sticks out all over the place and his blue-green baby eyes narrow at me suspiciously. His little fists curl around my beard and Poppy quickly steps in, trying to pry his tiny hands free. "Ta-ta, Quinn. We don't pull hair."

His grip tightens at the admonishment.

I raise an eyebrow. "Really, man, you gonna play like that?"

His squinty eyed stare gets even squintier. I swear this kid is one hundred percent his dad. I give him a little poke in the side and his eyes go wide before he giggles and his fists open. Poppy smiles and a flash goes off to my right. I glance over in time to see Lily tuck her phone in her back pocket.

The girls all head for the front door, murmuring excitedly about hair and nails and whatever other shit they're getting up to this afternoon. Lily pauses on her way down the hall. She gives Quinn a tickle under the chin and he bats his lashes at her. "Are you gonna be a good boy for Uncle Randy?"

He reaches for Lily and she takes his little tiny fist gently in her hand, pretending to nibble on his fingers. He giggles and buries his face against my chest, flirting shamelessly.

Lily's eyes go soft and her face takes on that wistful, faraway expression I've been seeing a lot more of lately.

If I'm going to be honest, it used to scare the fucking shit right out of me. I'd break out in the sweats and get all cagey. I tried not to, but it was like a conditioned response. One I didn't mean to have, but had a hard time hiding. Babies in general used to have the same effect.

But when almost all of your friends have kids and they're constantly passing them off to you like they believe you know what the fuck to do with them, you start to get used to it. And you kinda do learn how to handle them. It's a lot of trial and error from what I can tell.

Lily kisses Quinn on the cheek and then pushes up on her tiptoes. "Sorry I can't help you out, but I'll make it up to you later."

"You bet that sweet, sweet ass you will, Luscious."

She snorts indelicately.

"Such a romantic." She pats my cheek, bops Quinn on the nose and grabs her purse from the floor beside the coffee table. "You're sure you're gonna be okay?"

"My balls are already achy, but I'll survive."

"I mean with Quinn."

"Oh, yeah. It's half an hour, I got it handled." I hold up my hand in a high five and Quinn just stares at it.

"The boys will be here soon," Lily reassures me and then she follows Poppy down the hall to the front door.

I don't bother to follow her because the foyer is full of women trying to put their shoes on while they talk over each other about what color they want their nails, and I'm pretty sure Violet is talking about Vaggazling, which isn't something I want to know about. The door closes with a slam.

Quinn and I look at each other. His eyes have that wide, slightly panicked look about them. I'm pretty sure my expression must be similar.

The front door opens again. "I think I left my phone in the living room, give me a sec!" Violet comes rushing back in and almost trips over Wiener because she's looking over her shoulder instead of where she's going. She nearly does a face-plant into the floor and since I'm holding Quinn there's nothing I can do, so I watch helplessly as she stumbles and surprisingly recovers.

She blows out a breath. "Bite the bullet."

"What?"

She glances over her shoulder again and lowers her voice to a whisper. "This is me telling you it's time. She's ready."

"Are you talking about Lily?"

"Who else would I be talking about?"

"She's ready for what?" I'm super confused right now.

She rolls her eyes and sighs dramatically. "The white picket fence, you idiot." With that she spins around and disappears down the hall. The door slams shut again.

I glance down at Quinn who has his fingers in his mouth. "Did that make any sense to you?"

He squawks like an annoyed bird.

"Yeah, me either."

MILLER AND LANCE don't show up for almost an hour. By the time they arrive Quinn is having a massive meltdown and I have no idea why. I tried to feed him his bottle, I checked his diaper, and distracted him with some rattle thing, but nothing has worked so far.

Lance takes his screaming baby out of my arms. "It's all righ', Da's 'ere to save the day." He rummages around in the diaper bag until he finds a rubber giraffe and passes it to Quinn who promptly shoves the head in his mouth and starts gnawing on it. "He's teething. I'm surprised Poppy didn't say anything before she left."

"They were all a little preoccupied," I offer.

"I figured. Poppy was supposed to drop him off at Miller's before she came here, but she was a little scattered before she left this morning and ended up coming right here instead."

"Everything okay?" I ask.

"Aye. She just doesn't like to leave Quinn with the nanny for too long if she does 'nae have to, and he's been fussy lately 'cause 'o the teeth. Isn't that right, my little hellion?"

Quinn makes a sound somewhere between a gurgle and a giggle.

Once Quinn is no longer at risk of having another meltdown, Lance puts him in the playpen, turns on the hockey mobile, and we start setting up for the party. I'm distracted though, thinking about what Violet said.

"Earth to Balls," Miller snaps his fingers.

"Huh?" I stop rearranging the couch cushions.

"You've been doing that for three minutes. What's up?"

I drop the cushion. "Violet said something weird before the girls left today."

Miller snorts. "When doesn't Violet say something weird?"

I shrug. He has a point. "It was weirder than usual though, like she came back in to purposely relay the information, but it doesn't make any sense."

"It rarely does, but I have a lot of experience decoding the crap that comes out of her mouth if you want to run it by me," Miller offers.

"She told me Lily's ready and to bite the bullet." Miller doesn't say anything so I tack on. "Then she said *the white picket fence, you idiot* and left."

Miller and Lance exchange a look.

"Seriously, man?" Lance shakes his head and Miller rubs the back of his neck.

"What?"

"And here I thought Darren was the hopeless one," Lance mutters.

"She's talking about the ring," Miller says on a sigh.

"The ring?" I parrot.

Miller and Lance exchange another look.

I narrow my eyes at my best friend. Miller is the only person who knows about the ring. "What the hell is going on?"

Miller raises his hand. "Don't get mad."

"Did you tell Sunny about the ring?"

"Yeah. I mean, no. I mean, dude, she's my *wife*." Miller gives me an imploring look. "She shaves my balls for me, man."

"That's a lot of trust," Lance says stoically.

"She does a way better job than me," Miller adds.

"That's information I really didn't need." Especially since I've seen more of Miller's balls in my life than any best friend should. See the spider bite incident at camp a few years back for details. I do not want to think about the logistics of how Sunny shaving his balls would work, or what position he would need to be in for that to be effective. "What the hell happened to *I won't tell a soul*?"

"That never applies to wives," Lance defends Miller.

"You can't tell us that you don't tell Lily all the stuff you swear not to tell anyone else." Miller challenges me with an arched brow.

He's got me there.

"Anyway, Sunny promised not to say anything and I threatened to withhold cookie snacks if she did, not that I would actually follow through on the withholding, but I got your back, you know?" Miller grins, like this totally absolves him of his best friend betrayal. "Anyway, it's not like it matters now, 'cause Lily already found the ring and she told Sunny about it and Sunny told me, so that's how I know Violet is talking about the ring."

"Wait. Lily knows about the ring?"

Miller and Lance nod in tandem.

"For how long?"

They both shrug. "Dunno, a while, I guess?"

"A while?"

"Like maybe a month?" Miller adds.

"A month?" I stroke my beard, thinking about how things have been with Lily over the past four weeks leading up to her birthday, which incidentally is also around the holidays.

It's always kind of a tender time for us since I nearly fucked it all up back when we first started dating. Hooking up, actually, since I'd been convinced we couldn't be more than a fun time and casual bang-buddies.

I was such a fucking idiot.

And apparently I'm still an idiot because my girlfriend found the engagement ring I thought I'd done a good job of hiding a month ago and hasn't said a damn thing.

Eternally patient with me.

But it sure does explain the expectant look on her face every time I've said I had a question for her. It also explains that brief look of disappointment that followed whenever it was about mundane, stupid shit, or more often than not, whether she was interested in getting naked and bendy with me.

It takes a lot longer for all the pieces to fall into place than it should. I glance at the little tux Violet made for Wiener and the tiny cummerbund that fastens around his waist with the clip thing in the middle. The perfect place for a ring.

"I should propose tonight?"

"The set up is pretty ideal," Miller says with a shrug.

"You think she'll say yes?" Fuck. I'm suddenly really goddamn nervous.

Lance nods. "I think the odds are pretty good."

"Pretty good?"

"She'll say yes, she and Sunny have been looking at dresses a lot," Miller assures me.

"They have?"

"Yeah, but you have to keep your mouth shut about knowing that you know that she knows since I'm not supposed to know." Miller's face scrunches up, like what he's just said has confused him.

"Okay, tonight's the night, then."

THE GUYS LEAVE at four and Lily arrives home an hour later, kisses me on the cheek and rushes down the hall to the bedroom. I'm all of a minute behind her, because I don't want to look too eager and shit, but by the time I get there, she's locked herself in the bathroom.

I knock softly. "Luscious?"

"I just need a few minutes!" She calls out. The shower turns on.

"Uh, okay then?" No one is supposed to be here until six-thirty, so I have lots of time to make shit happen.

I dress poor Wiener up in his tux, apologizing for making him feel less than manly and tell him what the plan is for tonight. "I'm gonna ask your mom to marry me tonight and hopefully she's gonna say yes. Then you might have to wear this stupid penguin suit again for the wedding, 'cause you're kinda like our kid, yeah?"

He makes a pitiful sound.

I don't mention that there's a chance we might end up having an actual kid, because I don't want to stress him out more than he already is. Or I am. It's not as if I haven't thought about it. I have. A lot. It's hard not to when you're babysitting for your friends' kids and your girlfriend is always picking up tiny clothes and talking about how cute they are.

Lily would make a great mom. *Will* make a great mom. I know this because I see how she is with the kids she teaches skating lessons to and her nephews and our friends' little ones. She loves kids in general and takes every opportunity she can get to babysit. She'd never push me to have them because my own experience growing up was pretty damn shitty. But so was hers, and knowing that she'd give up the chance to have a family because she loves me makes me want to ensure she doesn't have to.

But first, I need to propose.

I put on my suit, because it's that kind of night, make sure my breath is fresh and my hair doesn't look like I've been running my hands through it and wait for Lily to come out of the bathroom.

Unfortunately, she stays locked in there for a really damn long time. At six I knock on the door. "You gonna be in there much longer, Luscious?"

"Almost finished!" she shouts. "Just a few more minutes."

I take a seat on the bed and wait. Wiener stands by my foot, tail wagging. I flip the little box between my sweaty fingers over and over.

Five minutes pass.

Wiener lowers his butt to the floor.

Eight.

Ten.

Wiener lies down and rests his chin on his paws.

Twelve.

"Luscious?" I call out.

"Just about ready!"

Wiener looks up at me, rolls over, and starts licking himself.

And of course the doorbell rings.

"Fuck," I mutter. So much for having something exciting to celebrate before our friends show up.

It turns out to be the caterer. I let them in so they can set up all the food in the dining room we never use apart from when we host parties. By the time everything is organized it's after six-thirty and people start to arrive.

Alex and Violet show up with Miller and Sunny. Violet gives me the eyeball. "Eh?"

"She's been locked in the bathroom since she got home," I mutter.

"Of course she has," Violet smirks and pats me on the shoulder. She and Sunny disappear in the direction of the bedrooms calling out for Lily.

"S'going on?" Alex asks.

"Balls is gonna pop the question tonight," Miller supplies.

"'Bout damn time." Alex claps me on the shoulder.

Two minutes later my girlfriend finally appears. If I thought my balls were achy before, it has nothing on how they feel now. Lily is wearing a very pretty, very short, very gauzy, sparkly champagne colored dress that was most definitely picked out with me in mind because it's very reminiscent of one of her skating outfits. I don't trust myself not to do something stupid like drag her into the bathroom and ruin the damn dress, so all I do is tell her she looks pretty and kiss her on the cheek before I leave her with the girls and get myself a beer. And a shot.

I spend most of the night trying to work up the nerve to just bite the bullet like Violet said, but I'm anxious as hell and Lily's . . . off. Like something's wrong and I don't know what it is. The last thing I want to do is pop the question when things are all wonky. So of course, that means I start second-guessing what the hell I'm doing.

Maybe Violet's wrong and she doesn't want the white picket fence.

Maybe Miller and Lance have it backwards.

Maybe she's getting tired of being with me.

I glance around the room, searching for her, but she's not standing with the girls.

"I'll be right back," I mutter to Miller, whose popping sausage puffs like an addict pops mollies.

I check the kitchen, but Lily's not there, she's not outside either—not that she would have a reason to be since the only thing out there is the beer cooler, and she's not in the garage getting more ice, or booze or whatever. I head down the hall, toward our bedroom.

I poke my head in and find her standing in front of our dresser, frantically searching my sock drawer. Which incidentally happens to be where I kept the ring until today.

I lean against the jamb and cross my arms. "Looking for something?"

She startles and slams the drawer shut, her wine glass tipping perilously. "You scared the shit out of me!" She grabs the glass with both hands—they're shaking—raises it to her mouth and takes a huge gulp.

"What're you doing?" I take a step inside the room and pull the door closed behind me.

Lily bites her lip. "I was just looking for . . . condoms."

"Why? We haven't used them in years." And when we did I kept them in the nightstand, not my sock drawer.

"Uh . . . Sunny was asking for some."

"I don't believe you." I flick the lock.

Her eyes dart around the room. She's definitely on the verge of . . . something. "We should get back out there." Her voice cracks.

I take a step closer and she fidgets with her wine glass, eyes fixed on the mostly empty glass.

I move into her personal space, take the glass and set it on the dresser again. I stroke along the edge of her jaw and tip her chin up. Her chocolate gaze meets mine and shifts quickly to the side. Her teeth sink into her bottom lip. "Luscious, what's going on?"

Her gaze is slow to return to mine. "I could ask you the same thing."

I arch a brow.

"You've been weird all night," she whispers.

"You came home and locked yourself in the bathroom for an hour and a half, so if we want to talk about acting weird, I think you win." I'm trying to be funny, but not.

Her fingers go to her mouth and then drop. Her chin trembles.

"Come on, Luscious, tell me what's going on?"

She lifts a shoulder and lets it fall.

Lily is a lot of things, but fragile is certainly not one of them, and right now she seems pretty damn breakable. Maybe she had too much to drink and has entered that weird state where women get all emotional about stuff.

Or maybe I'm a fucking idiot.

Because she came home after hours of pampering, rushed to our bedroom and then promptly made it impossible for me to get to her until our company arrived. And then I find her in here, going through my sock drawer, apparently looking for condoms we don't use.

I might be a little drunk. Not a lot drunk, but enough that I'm more clueless than usual.

I slip my hand inside my suit jacket and pull out the tiny Tiffany's box. "Is this what you were looking for?"

Lily's eyes go wide, and dart from the box to my face, like she's watching a tennis match on a very tiny TV screen. Several emotions cross her face: embarrassment, relief, fear. I don't understand that last one until my dumbass brain finally puts everything together.

Such as the fact that I've had this ring for months and I've been trying to find the balls to ask her, and that she found it a month ago and has been sitting on that information this entire time, waiting for me to pop the damn question, and that today the ring disappeared, likely making her wonder if I changed my mind.

"I love the fuck out of you," I tell her. "And into you." I cringe because that was bad. "I love you. More than anything else in the entire goddamn universe, including hockey."

She smiles and laughs a little, but that wateriness in her eyes doesn't go away, in fact, two tears leak out and trail slowly down her cheeks. She dashes them away. "I love you more than figure skating," she whispers.

"I know we said we didn't need the labels, but I kinda want it now. I'm going to love you for the rest of your life and I want to put a ring on it, you know?" Geez I suck at proposals. And to think I practiced this like five thousand times in my head. None of them went this badly. Maybe cue cards would've been a good idea. "We don't have to have a big wedding or anything. It can just be like a backyard thing with our friends and our families. I just want you to be mine. Forever. Officially."

She blinks up at me smiling softly.

I blink down at her. Waiting.

A lot of seconds pass. Or it feels like a lot of seconds. Maybe it's just a few.

"You have to ask for me to say yes," she says gently.

"Oh! Shit! Right." I drop to one knee in front of her, take her hand in mine and flip open the box. The diamond glints in the light. It's pretty modest as far as diamonds go because I didn't want to be too ostentatious about it and Lily isn't big on flash.

"Lily, I never thought I'd find someone like you, and now that I have you I don't ever want to let you go, and I mean that in the most non-psychotic way possible. Please marry me?" I clamp my mouth shut and wait so I don't mess it up more than I already have.

"I'd love to marry you." Her smile makes the tightness in my chest dissipate.

"For real?" I hope she's not just saying yes because our friends are here.

"Of course."

"You don't have to take my last name or anything, but I wouldn't be opposed if you wanted to." I slide the ring onto her finger. It's a perfect fit. "And if you're game I wouldn't mind knocking you up eventually, 'cause you'd be a kickass mom and I think I could probably handle being a dad, but we can revisit that later, in like, three to five years or whenever makes the most sense."

Lily takes my face in her hands and bends to kiss me, which is good because I'm Violet-style word vomiting all my thoughts at her and I'd like this to be memorable for reasons other than me being an ass.

"I love you," she whispers against my lips.

"I love you, too." I use the edge of the dresser to help me to my feet. "Did you think I changed my mind when you couldn't find the ring?"

"I don't know what I thought." She wraps her hand around the back of my neck when I lift her onto the dresser and step between her parted thighs. "But I'm glad I was wrong."

"You're my only, Luscious." It's a promise I intend to keep forever.

"And you're mine."

I drop my mouth to hers and she parts her lips, welcoming me in. She tastes like a fruity cocktail I can't get enough of. Lily threads her fingers through my hair and locks her legs around my waist so we rub all up on each other like we're trying to start a fire with our sex parts.

Our friends are pretty used to us disappearing in the middle of parties, and if there was ever a time for sex-ebrating, getting engaged is it. I kiss my way along the side of her neck and find the zipper on the back of her dress, tugging it down. The fabric slips over her shoulders, exposing her perky breasts. She's not wearing a bra, so her nipples are covered with Band-Aids to prevent them from being visible through her dress. I carefully peel the adhesive away and cover the pert nipple with my mouth, circle it with my tongue before I suck gently.

Lily arches and sighs, one hand staying in my hair, the other reaching for my belt buckle. Inside of a minute the top of her dress is pooled at her waist, her panties are on the floor and she's stroking my achy erection in her fist—with the hand that now bears a diamond ring.

We stop kissing and both drop our gazes to watch her palm glide along my cock, thumb sweeping over the tip, dragging the wetness along my shaft on the down stroke.

"We'll make this our appetizer round?" She strokes twice more.

I nod, completely enthralled with watching her hand moving over me. I push the skirt of her dress up and tuck the loose fabric into the top, slipping my fingers between her parted thighs. I drag a knuckle along her slit, teasing her clit before I go lower and push inside with two fingers.

Lily clenches immediately, eyes falling closed and lips parting on a soft sigh. It's always been like this with us, and despite all the years together, our appetite for each other has never diminished. Her grip around my shaft loosens when I find that place inside that makes her shudder.

When it feels like she's hovering on the edge of an orgasm, I withdraw my fingers, intent on replacing them with my cock. We both exhale on a low groan as I fill her up. I ease my hips back and surge forward, making all the things on the dresser rattle.

We both make a face, glancing at the perfume bottle that tipped over.

Her knees clamp against my hips, feet hooked behind my back, fingers linked behind my neck and without a word I lift her off the dresser and carry her into the bathroom, depositing her on the vanity so we can fuck-ebrate our engagement without tipping off our company or breaking anything.

Besides, our bathroom has a lot of mirrors, which means we have a fantastic view from every single angle. We watch my cock disappear inside her with every fast, hard stroke and it doesn't take long for her eyes to roll up as she contracts around me. I hold off as long as I can, wanting to savor this new first before I follow behind her, the orgasm rolling through me, stealing my coordination.

I drop my forehead to her shoulder and twist my head so my lips meet her skin, her pulse frantic beneath my lips.

She runs her fingers through my hair. "After everyone leaves you're going to fuck me into oblivion, right?"

I lift my head, taking in her flushed face and the mischievous glint in her eyes. "Damn right, I am. This night is ending in beard rides and a shit-ton of orgasms."

Lily smirks. "And we should probably make a video . . . you know . . . for celebratory purposes."

"That was pretty much a given." I take her hand in mine and kiss the knuckle above her new ring. The one that says she's unequivocally mine, and I'm hers. "Thank you for being patient."

"I know I'm your only in every way that counts." Her smile softens and she presses her hand over my heart. "Label or no label, that's all that's ever mattered."

ABOUT THE AUTHOR

NYT and USA Today bestselling author, Helena Hunting lives on the outskirts of Toronto with her amazing family and her two awesome cats, who think the best place to sleep is her keyboard. Helena writes everything from emotional contemporary romance to romantic comedies that will have you laughing until you cry. If you're looking for a tearjerker, you can find her angsty side under H. Hunting.

Scan this code to stay connected with Helena

OTHER TITLES BY HELENA HUNTING

Pucked Series

Pucked (Pucked #1)

Pucked Up (Pucked #2)

Pucked Over (Pucked #3)

Forever Pucked (Pucked #4)

Pucked Under (Pucked #5)

Pucked Off (Pucked #6)

Pucked Love (Pucked #7)

AREA 51: Deleted Scenes & Outtakes

Get Inked

Pucks & Penalties

All In Series

A Lie for a Lie

A Favor for a Favor

A Secret for a Secret

A Kiss for a Kiss

Lies, Hearts & Truths Series

Little Lies

Bitter Sweet Heart

Shattered Truths

Standalone Novels

The Librarian Principle

Felony Ever After

Before You Ghost (with Debra Anastasia)

Forever Romance Standalones

The Good Luck Charm

Meet Cute

Kiss my Cupcake

Printed in Great Britain
by Amazon

41919315R00116